THE MOON KILLER

An enthralling murder mystery with a twist

FRANCES LLOYD

Detective Inspector Jack Dawes Mystery Book 5

JOFFE BOOKS

First published 2020
Joffe Books, London
www.joffebooks.com

Please join our mailing list for free Kindle books and new releases.

ISBN 978-1-78931-390-1

CHAPTER ONE

20 March. The Worm Moon

Wayne Jenkins slammed the door of the Goat and Garter behind him and locked it. Outside, the night air hit him, cold and dank after the hot, stuffy pub. He paused under a street lamp to light a cigarette, inhaled deeply, and was seized by a fit of coughing. It was miserable enough running a pub at the best of times, but doing it without a fag was inhuman. It had been a busy night and profitable in more ways than one. He looked at the watch that he'd bought from a punter earlier that evening. It was twenty past one. The bloke reckoned it was a Rolex, but Wayne doubted it, not for a tenner anyway.

A lot of moody gear changed hands in the pub on Friday nights and enough drugs to space out the whole of Kings Richington. Jenkins turned a blind eye, the same eye that was on constant alert for any unwelcome attention from coppers. He could spot the filth a mile off. He'd had his collar felt several times and the licence was always under threat. It hadn't curbed his criminal activities though, just made him more vigilant. But recently, he'd seen a chance to make some real money. All right, it was risky — very risky, he knew that. But small-time crooks made small-time money. Time to move up a league, several leagues in fact. If everything worked out and he kept his nerve, he'd soon be out of this skanky pub and living the high life somewhere sunny.

It was starting to drizzle and he still had a good twenty-minute walk across the park to his council flat. Time was, he'd have done it in ten, but he wasn't so fit now. Too many fags and fry-ups. As a skinny young footballer, he'd trained hard, so he could put away all the burgers and beer he'd liked and still been able to sprint up the wing and put the ball in the back of the net before the goalie even saw him coming. He reckoned he had to be at least five stone fatter now, and his lungs weren't up to much.

But it didn't really matter what he looked like or how long it took him to get home — there was nobody waiting up for him. His wife, sick of his dodgy dealings, dirty habits and general lack of any redeeming features, had kicked him out once the kids were grown. Not that it mattered now. With the kind of money he was planning to make, he could have any woman he wanted. He fancied a little Thai girl or maybe a Filipino. Someone who'd do as she was told without nagging. He'd soon teach her. He turned up the collar of his greasy jacket and set off.

Even with the full moon, the park was pitch black, but Jenkins had walked it so many times he could find his way with his eyes shut. The shortest route took him across the grass, around the flower beds, and through a dense shrubbery which eventually came out by the lake. At that hour and in the pouring rain he didn't expect to meet anyone; he rarely did. It was when he reached the shrubbery that he heard the rustling and sensed something was in there. He wasn't going to call out, 'Hello, is anybody there?' like a big, frightened girl, and it was probably only some animal anyway. All the same, he stopped and listened.

The blow came out of nowhere, like a sledgehammer driving deep into his fat, flabby belly. One strike was all it needed. He staggered backwards, twisted around and fell face down in the lake. And who knows how long he would have stayed there, hidden in the reeds, if it hadn't been for Agnes Littlewood and her chihuahua, Daisy.

* * *

Detective Sergeant 'Bugsy' Malone of the London Metropolitan Murder Investigation Team was not at all happy. This weather wasn't fit for dogs to be out in, never mind a copper. The rain was relentless, almost horizontal. Reluctantly, he struggled out of his car, bracing his considerable bulk against the storm. The wind snatched the door from his grasp and slammed it shut, trapping the end of his Arsenal scarf. He cursed. Another ten minutes and he'd have been in the Richington Arms and out of radio contact. By now, he should be sitting in the convivial warmth of the bar with a pie and a pint. Instead, he was plodding across Richington Park, where Detective Constable Williams claimed there had been a suspicious death. Malone turned up his collar and grumbled, silently. If it turned out to be just another tramp who had drunk himself to death on a park bench, he would not be pleased. The newly promoted DC was a good lad but altogether too keen on chasing crime for Bugsy's liking.

The rain had been lashing down all day and now, at seven in the evening, the storm was still raging. Richington Park was boggy, particularly around the lake, where police tape flapped jauntily in the wind, marking the location of a far from jaunty corpse. Malone wondered if he should have changed into the wellingtons he kept in the car, but they were buggers to get on, particularly when your socks were already wet. Unwilling to battle with the boot of his car in the gale, he'd decided against it. Two minutes and twenty yards later, he realized it was a mistake. He could feel the sludge squelching through the lace holes of his trainers. Already, his Arsenal scarf was sodden, the fringes whipping round in the gale and slapping him in the face like cold tagliatelle. A uniformed constable lifted the tape for him to duck underneath and he trudged across to where DC Aled

Williams was crouched over the body, going through the pockets.

'This had better be good, Taffy. I was on my way to an important meeting with a pie and a pint in the Richington Arms.'

Williams stood up. 'Sorry, Sarge. The DI wasn't answering his mobile. I've put a call out for him.'

Malone grinned. 'Never mind, son. I dare say his missus was trying out one of her recipes on him. Who's this poor bugger?' He indicated the dead man lying face down in the pond.

'This is Wayne Jenkins. He is — was — the landlord of the Goat and Garter in Lower Richington, a sleazy pub in the worst part of town. He's well known to the police for allowing out of hours drinking, suspected drug dealing, receiving stolen goods and other petty crimes, although we've never been able to make anything stick. We've arrested him a few times, so we have his DNA on file, but he's never been charged.'

'Who found the body?' Bugsy nursed the fond hope that the person who'd found the dead body was the killer, which would make life very much simpler. He'd even been right, once.

'A little old lady, walking her chihuahua.'

'In this weather? She must have been soaked.'

'She was, Sarge. The dog fell in the lake, got caught up in the reeds and, fearing it might drown, she waded in to rescue it. She tripped over the dead man's legs in the dark. Fortunately, she managed to keep her phone dry and called the police.'

This confirmed Bugsy's long-held belief that all dog owners were barmy, especially the ones who sprinted about the countryside with their mutts, falling over dead bodies. If he'd had a pound for the number of times it had happened, he could have retired a rich man by now. He glanced around.

'Where is she now?'

'I sent her home in a police car, Sarge.' DC Gemma Fox plodded through the mud towards him. 'The poor soul was shivering. So was her dog.'

'She's not the only one.' Malone wrung out the ends of his Arsenal scarf. He never left home without it, so it was tatty and bedraggled, even on a good day. 'What made you call it in as a suspicious death? It could've been an accident,' he said, more in hope than expectation. 'The bloke is seriously fat and was probably intoxicated, lucky bugger; I can smell the booze on him from here. What if he was taking a short cut across the park in crappy footwear . . .' Malone indicated the worn trainers, '. . . he stumbles in the mud, falls and bashes his head on one of those paving slabs. Ends up face down in the pond and drowns. What d'you reckon?' The siren call of steak and kidney pie and double chips beckoned.

Detective Inspector Jack Dawes loomed out of the dusk, his six foot three frame towering over the crime scene. He wasn't happy, either. Water was dripping from his raincoat collar and down his neck. 'I just got the call. What have we got, Bugsy?'

'Evening, guv. Nice weather for it.' Malone stood back so that Dawes could examine the scene.

Jack chewed his lip, thoughtfully. He squatted down, the better to see the dead man's injuries. Why did these incidents always happen where there's no CCTV?

'There's no blood on his head or on the paving slabs, Bugsy. I guess the rain could have washed it away. Has anyone called the pathologist?'

Doctor Veronica Hardacre was privately nicknamed Big Ron because of her imposing height and girth, and her reputation for taking no prisoners. She was surly and aggressive, but brilliant at her job and a stickler for following procedure. By the time she'd finished poking and prodding around, putting things in evidence bags and muttering to herself, Bugsy would be left with just pie crumbs to go with his pint.

'Good evening, Detective Inspector Dawes.' The ringing tones of Dr Hardacre came from behind, followed by a strong whiff of formaldehyde. The pathologist was wrestling with a large golfing umbrella, which she attempted to hold over herself and her bag of tricks, which accompanied her pretty much everywhere. It was rumoured that nobody in the police service had ever questioned her judgement and survived unscathed. In particular, she had scant regard for senior police officers who pre-empted her findings, considering themselves more knowledgeable than the due process of science.

She crouched to inspect the body. It was some time before she finally stood up and addressed Dawes again.

'Before you ask, a definitive time of death will be difficult, due to this appalling weather. Even after I get him back to the mortuary, there is likely to be a wide margin of probability. At a guess, I'd say the poor devil has been lying here for at least twelve to sixteen hours. I'll arrange for the body to be taken away.'

'Did he drown, Dr Hardacre?' asked Malone.

The pathologist gave him a surprised look, as if seeing him for the first time. 'I've absolutely no idea.' She turned to Dawes. 'Post-mortem at eight thirty sharp tomorrow morning. I'll have cause of death then. Good evening.' She squelched back through the mud, her hair, never her best feature, hanging in lank grey tendrils, despite the umbrella.

Once the body had been removed, Sergeant Malone plodded away to see if there was any hot food left in the pub. Jack climbed into his car and drove back home for a hot bath and his unfinished dinner. He had left a warm kitchen where his wife, Corrie Dawes, was trying out a new recipe for osso buco with saffron risotto. She owned 'Coriander's Cuisine,' a lucrative catering business, and had recently branched out into 'Corrie's Kitchen,' an online meal delivery service. She had a small staff of mostly young people anxious to make their way in hospitality, and from time to time, she would try out a new meal on Dawes before she unleashed it upon her customers. She also took a keen interest in his murder cases — a bit too keen in Dawes's view — and had, during their marriage, got herself into some quite dangerous scrapes as a result. Dawes had only swallowed a forkful of risotto when he'd got the call earlier.

Corrie had managed to preserve the meal to almost pristine excellence. She hung his raincoat in the porch where it created a sizeable puddle. There was a manky old football scarf hanging out of the pocket.

'Is this yours, darling?' She held it up.

'No,' said Jack. 'It belongs to Bugsy. He left it behind at the crime scene.'

'I didn't know Bugsy was a Chelsea fan,' said Corrie. When DS Malone had joined the police, a service notorious for assigning nicknames to colleagues, he had inevitably been called 'Bugsy,' after the film, and it had stuck. Now, nobody could remember his real name; it was doubtful whether he could himself. It was the same with 'Jack' Dawes, whose real first name was Rupert.

'He isn't,' said Jack. 'It's an Arsenal scarf, darling. He always wears it. I thought you would have recognized the Arsenal colours, being a London girl.'

'Certainly not.' Corrie pulled a face. 'I don't "do" football. I don't like the laddish behaviour attached to it,' she declared, sipping her Chardonnay. 'I'd ban it, drive it underground like bareknuckle fighting. It's just publicly endorsed, yobbish hooliganism. I don't believe men evolved from apes to stand in crowds, shouting mindlessly and chanting.' She topped up her glass and reached for a parmesan crisp, one of her new canapé lines. 'Did you know, watching football lowers men's IQs by about one hundred points — and these are points they can ill afford to lose.'

Jack laughed. 'I don't believe you.'

'There's plenty of evidence. How many times during a match do you hear men shout at the TV? *"Messi, shoot, you numpty!"* Messi can't hear them. And even if he could, why would one of the highest-earning footballers in the world pay the slightest bit of attention to a fat, crisp-crunching armchair critic?'

'The only men you'll find who don't like football,' said Jack, wiping sauce from his top lip, 'are the ones who were never picked for the team at school.'

'I see. So, all males are genetically wired to fall in love with the beautiful game and the few who don't are physically inadequate, the sporting underclass. Is that what you honestly believe, Jack?'

'Don't ask me. Rugby was my game. Used to play wing half. Bloody good I was, too. Mind, there is the psychological argument that football lets off steam in aggressive, testosterone-driven young males.'

'On the contrary, I think it can actually create it,' said Corrie. She was to remember the shocking relevance of this observation many times during the following months.

CHAPTER TWO

The post-mortem revealed that while Wayne Jenkins had a considerable amount of alcohol in his blood, he had not taken a drunken fall and accidentally knocked himself unconscious. And contrary to DS Malone's suggestion, he hadn't drowned, either. The actual cause of death astonished even the pathologist who, after thirty years in the business, was rarely shocked by any bizarre atrocity that one human being could inflict upon another.

The mortuary room was ice cold, with dazzling white tiles and a cloying, antiseptic smell that caught in Jack's throat, leaving an acrid aftertaste of something nasty, like a cheap cabernet sauvignon. Reluctantly, he joined DS Malone, DC Fox and DC Williams, gowned up and waiting beside the naked cadaver on the table, which appeared even more bloated and obscene than it had in the park.

Dr Hardacre stood at the head of the corpse wearing, as was her custom, the complete autopsy kit — cap, mask, plain goggles, gumboots and gloves reaching up to the elbows. Her assistant, Miss Catwater, in similar garb, stood at her elbow making notes.

'Death occurred sometime between two and four o'clock in the morning, some sixteen hours before the body was discovered. The victim suffered a substantial blow to the abdomen which ruptured several of his vital organs. I can find no evidence of a weapon, so it is my opinion that the perpetrator delivered the powerful blow using his fist or foot. It was dark, in spite of the full moon, and the victim had sufficient alcohol in his blood to impair his sensibility. In other words, it is unlikely that he even saw the attack coming let alone the person responsible.'

'So he was rendered unconscious by a vicious punch or kick to the gut?' suggested Dawes.

'And then the poor sod fell face down in the lake and drowned,' finished Malone.

Dr Hardacre shook her head. 'Wrong in both cases, gentlemen. This is what killed our unfortunate friend.' She held out her hand and Miss Catwater obediently handed her a kidney dish. The pathologist thrust it under the police officers' noses with a theatrical flourish. All four peered at the contents in puzzled silence, until Malone coughed, awkwardly. 'Isn't that a . . . ? I mean, surely it wouldn't . . .'

Jack frowned. 'Is that what I think it is?'

'Aren't they those things that women . . . ?' DC Williams hesitated.

'It's a tampon,' announced Gemma Fox, bluntly.

'Correct, young lady. It is indeed an item of internal feminine sanitary hygiene. It had been rammed so far down the victim's throat that I nearly missed it. While there is every possibility that the deceased would have died rapidly from his internal injuries, and indeed could have drowned, the fact remains that he was dead before either of those eventualities could take place. The tampon swelled up and choked him.'

'But why would anyone do such a thing?' Jack asked. 'That's a grotesque way to kill a man.'

Dr Hardacre nodded. 'In my experience, most murders are grotesque, Inspector Dawes, but finding out why this one happened is your job. I believe I have done mine. Miss

Catwater will have my report on your desk this afternoon. Good day, officers.'

* * *

Back at the station, Dawes disappeared to brief the Chief Super, leaving the troops to begin digging for information on Wayne Jenkins that might lead them to find out who killed him in such a bizarre manner.

According to Sergeant Parsloe, uniform knew him well. 'He was a small-time low-life scrote. Treated his wife like shit for years until she had the sense to kick him out. None of his family wanted anything to do with him and he didn't have any friends, apart from the crooks who used his pub for criminal activities. He was a fat, smelly waste of oxygen.'

Bugsy grinned. 'So what you're trying to say, in your typically understated and impartial manner, Norman, is that it won't be hard to find suspects who didn't like him.'

Norman grunted. 'Hard to find anyone who did.'

'Surely, he wasn't like that all his life,' said Aled, who was still young enough to believe there was some good in the hardest of criminals. 'Was he in trouble when he was young?'

'No, he wasn't, as it happens,' he conceded. 'He was a pretty good footballer as a youngster — a striker for Richington United. I believe he even got a trial with one of the London clubs. But the booze and fags and parties got to him and he stopped putting in the training, so they dropped him.'

Bugsy was impressed. 'Norman, mate, you're a mine of information. But we really need to find out what he was up to recently rather than — what must it be — twenty years ago? I doubt if anyone with a grudge would wait that long to get even.'

'What about next of kin?' asked Gemma. 'Shouldn't we notify someone?'

PC Simon Jackson looked up from the police database on his screen. 'According to his record, he was divorced from

Sandra Jenkins five years ago, but we have an address on file for her.' Jackson, a fast track psychology and criminology graduate, had been newly assigned to assist MIT following the promotion of PC Aled Williams to Detective Constable. He was keen to get on, as quickly as possible. 'Jenkins had a grown-up son, Ronald, and a daughter, but we don't have any details for her.'

'Right,' said Malone. 'Gemma and I will go and see Mrs Jenkins, and Mitch, you have a poke around Jenkins's flat and the Goat and Garter and see if anyone knows anything. Or, more to the point, if you can get anyone to talk. Take Jackson with you.' He winked. 'It'll give him a chance to see the glamourous side of our job.'

DC 'Mitch' Mitchell was a safe pair of hands. He was older than the other detective constables in the team and balanced their enthusiasm and impulsiveness with sound judgement and experience.

* * *

Sandra Jenkins lived in a terraced council house in Lower Richington, not the most salubrious part of Kings Richington but not the rough end either. According to police data, she was thirty-nine, but DC Fox thought she looked at least ten years older. She reckoned that was what an abusive marriage did to a woman, never mind having a child at sixteen and another only two years later.

Bugsy explained as tactfully as he could that her husband had been found dead without revealing any of the unpleasant details. She showed no emotion but they had been divorced for five years, so she was hardly likely to burst into tears. All the same, you never knew how people would react.

'What was it — his heart?' she asked. 'I was forever telling him if he didn't leave off the fags, the fry-ups and the drink, it would catch up with him. He never listened, just accused me of nagging.'

'No, it wasn't his heart, Mrs Jenkins. We believe your ex-husband was murdered.'

She caught her breath at that and sat down suddenly on a kitchen chair.

'Would you like me to make you a cup of tea, Mrs Jenkins?' asked Gemma.

Before she could answer, the back door opened and a stocky young man came in, obviously a younger and fitter version of Wayne Jenkins. He looked around at the police presence.

'You all right, Ma?'

'Yes, I'm fine, son. Just had a bit of a shock, that's all. It's your dad. These police officers say he's been murdered.'

The way Malone saw it, you didn't have to be Sherlock Holmes to deduce that Ronald Jenkins wasn't as shocked as he might have been to hear that someone had bumped off his father.

'We'll need someone to come and formally identify Mr Jenkins. Would that be possible, Mrs Jenkins?'

'I'll do it, Ma.' Ronald put his arm around her. 'You don't have to go.' He looked enquiringly at DS Malone. 'She don't have to do it, does she? She had enough of the sod when he was alive; she shouldn't 'ave to be bovvered by 'im now he's dead.'

'No, that will be fine. We could give you a lift to the mortuary now, if that would be convenient.'

'Yeah, let's get it over wiv.'

Bugsy thought it odd that neither mother nor son had asked how Jenkins had died or where he was found. This could either mean they were beyond caring or that they already knew. In any event, he wasn't about to volunteer the information.

* * *

Back in the chilly, white-tiled mortuary, the mortuary assistant removed the sheet. Ronald Jenkins glanced at the body and nodded. 'Yeah, that's Dad. Can I go now?'

'I wonder if you'd mind telling us a bit about your father, Mr Jenkins. It might help us find out who killed him.'

DC Fox wondered exactly what he did know and whether he was likely to offer any information. There was clearly no love lost between father and son. 'We'll give you a lift home afterwards. Perhaps a cup of tea?'

In the interview room, Ronald Jenkins dipped the custard cream in the tea DC Fox had given him and slurped it noisily. They'd already established that he was a plumber by trade and lived with his pregnant girlfriend in the council house next door but one to his mum.

'Can you think of anyone who might want to harm your father, Mr Jenkins? We know he managed the Goat and Garter public house. Did he have any enemies?' Sergeant Malone watched for a reaction, expecting the man to declare his father a paragon of virtue who'd never had an enemy in his life and had a wonderful sense of humour. That was the usual response when a relative died. But Jenkins hesitated and stared down at his hands.

'I used to drop in there for a drink some nights. Never said nothing to me mum, cause she didn't like me seeing Dad. Said he was trouble, always would be, and I should steer clear. He was the reason me sister left home. He beat up 'er boyfriend bad enough to put him in hospital. I guess she'd have a reason to want him dead but she's in New Zealand. But he was me dad, after all.' He took another slurp of tea. 'Thing is, he was making money on the side. That pub is always full of low lifes on the take.'

'We know he handled stolen goods,' said DC Williams. 'He'd been arrested a couple of times. But hardly serious enough to warrant his murder.'

Jenkins shook his head. 'No, I don't mean shiftin' moody merchandise. It was more than that.'

'Drugs?' asked Malone. 'The word on the street is that the Goat and Garter is the place to go and your dad turned a blind eye.'

'Yeah, but he didn't just turn a blind eye, did he? He was the one supplying the gear in the first place.'

Bugsy raised an expressive eyebrow. 'Do you know where he got it from?'

'No, I bloody well don't, and I don't want to know either! What I do know is that Dad used to take delivery for one of the big city boys, but before he handed it over, he creamed some off the top and cut the rest with cornflour to make up the weight. Then he pushed what he'd nicked in the pub.'

'Bloody hell!' Malone swore under his breath. 'Dangerous game, that.'

'That's what I told 'im. Top you soon as look at you, if you double-cross those blokes.'

* * *

DC Mitchell and PC Jackson sauntered up to the bar in the Goat and Garter. Mitch wore corduroys and a casual jacket, Simon was in jeans and a hoodie. To an untrained eye, they could have been father and son, out for a lunchtime drink. However, the replacement landlord installed by the brewery did not have an untrained eye.

'Afternoon, officers. What can I get you?'

Simon was surprised. He'd thought they looked completely random, nothing at all like police officers. But Mitch knew blokes in pubs like this could spot a copper a mile off, even in plain clothes. He'd often wondered whether it was the way they walked or just a certain smell of the law. No point denying it or pretending you were an estate agent or something. They always knew. He ordered two orange juices.

'Did you know Wayne Jenkins, the previous landlord here?' Mitchell sipped his drink.

The man began wiping up slops with a cloth filthier than the bar. 'Yeah, I knew him. It was always me who was put in as relief whenever he was ill. Guess I've got the job permanent now he's gone.'

'Was he ill very often?' asked Simon.

He hesitated. 'Yeah, well, he didn't have a very healthy lifestyle, if you get my drift.'

'Well, we know he wasn't very fit and he smoked and drank heavily,' said Simon. 'Is that what you mean?'

'Nah, it was the beatings mostly. Always had a black eye or his arm in a sling. Was that what did for 'im in the end? I never heard what killed 'im.'

'Who gave him the beatings?' Mitchell reckoned they might be onto something, but sensing he might have said too much, the man clammed up instantly.

'Couldn't tell you, squire. He never said and I never asked. But I know they put 'im in hospital more than once.'

It was obvious they weren't going to find out anything more and as Mitch often said, there's a limit to how much orange juice a man can drink before it strips the enamel off his teeth.

A look round Jenkins's flat was equally unproductive. It was grimy, stark and unwelcoming, with soiled clothes thrown on the floor and dirty dishes in the sink. It stank of tobacco, booze and stale sweat. They poked about for a bit, then Simon said, 'Look at these, Mitch.'

On a shelf in the bedroom, there were a number of cups and statuettes of footballers. A certificate on the wall had the Richington United crest with a photograph of a young, fit Jenkins underneath.

'Sergeant Parsloe was right. It says Jenkins was Under-21 Striker of the Year.'

'Didn't end well, though, did it? Come on, there's nothing here. Let's get back to the station.'

* * *

The general consensus of the team, and most people who'd had any dealings with Jenkins, was that he had got what he deserved. All the same, it was a murder, contrary to common law, and it was their job to investigate and catch the killer.

'Strikes me, Jenkins was asking for it,' mumbled Bugsy, chewing the last of his pork pie lunch. 'If you sup with city drug barons, you need a bloody long spoon. Daresay the top man found out he was being ripped off and made an example of Jenkins to stop anyone else trying the same game.'

'Bit harsh, Sarge,' observed Aled.

'Yeah, well, they weren't likely to give him a slap on the wrist and tell him not to do it again, were they? They've got their reputations to think of.'

'*Pour encourager les autres*,' agreed DC Fox.

'No, I don't think they were French, Gemma,' said Aled. 'I believe most of the hard stuff comes from places like Colombia and Pakistan.'

Gemma smiled. 'Yes, of course. Silly me.'

'Why use a tampon as the murder weapon?' Simon had studied some seriously sick behaviour during his psychology degree, but this was beyond gross. 'Why not just shoot or stab the bloke, gangland style? Much quicker and less messy.'

'And why wait until the dead of night, during a downpour and hidden away in the park?' asked Bugsy. 'If the intention was to put it out there as a punishment execution, you'd do it somewhere other criminals were sure to see it.'

Over the next weeks, the team established possible motives and questioned many potential suspects, but evidence was sparse and opportunity even worse. Jenkins's last known sighting for pretty much everyone was in the Goat and Garter that night. Finally, almost a month later, the intelligence they thought they had was turned completely on its head by a second murder.

CHAPTER THREE

19 April. The Pink Moon

The Bryce-Jones Investment Company occupied several floors of a light-filled skyscraper located on Canary Wharf. It boasted far-reaching views over London's Docklands, which impressed its many foreign investors. This stylish location formed the hub of many banking and finance businesses and was ideally situated for making a lot of money.

Toby Bryce-Jones parked his BMW in the space labelled 'Company Director' and made his way to the lift. His wife, Camilla, had taken the Range Rover to transport their two daughters to an Easter swimming gala. They had left very early so Toby had only had orange juice and coffee for breakfast.

He reached his office at precisely nine o'clock, as he always did. He was a man who needed routine and consistency in his life in order to function properly. When he reached the office, he would always go directly to the executive washroom to wash his hands and check his appearance. Today, being Good Friday, most of his staff were on holiday, but he was expecting some important Arab investors from Dubai and since Easter was not a holiday for them, it wasn't for him either.

On his way to the washroom, he passed the office of his personal assistant. He put his head around the door.

'Caroline, do you think you could send out for some coffee and croissants? I missed breakfast and I'm expecting a deputation from the Dubai International Finance Centre in half an hour. I need some serious carbs.'

'Yes, of course, Mr Bryce-Jones. The meeting room is all set out for you.' She ordered the croissants and carried on with her work. A determined career woman, in what was a predominantly male environment, she had no problem with working over Easter.

Half an hour later, when Bryce-Jones had not reappeared, she showed the deputation of Arab gentlemen into the meeting room. The croissants in Bryce-Jones's office were now cold, despite being wrapped in a napkin. Caroline decided to go and look for him. The key to the men's washroom was still in the door, but she was apprehensive about barging in. One of the cleaners, who had been in overnight, was putting her trolley away in a nearby cupboard, anxious to get home to buy Easter eggs for her children.

Caroline approached her. 'Hilda, before you go, do you think you might just pop into the executive washroom for me and see if Mr Bryce-Jones is still there? He went in half an hour ago and I haven't seen him come back out. I can see the washroom from my desk, so I'd know if he'd gone anywhere else. I'd be very grateful, only there are some important businessmen waiting for him.'

Hilda wondered whether the poor man had some kind of bowel problem. Diarrhoea could be very debilitating, even for a company director. She put her sign outside — 'female operative in attendance' — and went in, calling out, 'Are you in here, Mr Bryce-Jones?'

There was no answer and it seemed empty. Then she noticed that the door of the end cubicle was closed. Maybe the boss was in there. So why didn't he answer? She knocked on the door. Still nothing. The door wasn't locked so she pushed it open, hoping she wouldn't find him sitting on the loo with his trousers around his ankles. He was sitting on the seat, fully clothed and very dead.

* * *

Detective Chief Superintendent Garwood strode into the incident room wearing that purposeful expression that indicated he had something important to say and everyone had better listen up. The team was grouped around the whiteboard, which had precious little on it, despite the many hours spent sifting through the seedy life and even seedier death of Wayne Jenkins. They had investigated his known associates, his habits and his last hours but, truthfully, they were no further forward. He had been such a low life that anyone might have had a motive.

'Leave that,' ordered Garwood, waving at the board. 'This new case takes top priority. I've just been informed by the Commander, Sir Barnaby, that the body of Toby Bryce-Jones has been discovered.' He paused, waiting for exclamations of shock and horror, but none came, so he continued. 'Those of you who dabble on the stock market will recognize his name as the head of a very lucrative and successful investment company. Indeed, I have, on occasion, taken advantage of his advice myself — in a purely modest way, of course and in no contravention of the police code of ethics.'

'Was he a close friend, sir?' enquired DI Dawes. He seriously doubted whether anyone on the Murder Investigation Team apart from Garwood had the time or the money to gamble in stocks and shares, never mind the market knowledge.

'No, not close, Dawes,' said Garwood, irritably. 'My wife, Cynthia, and I have occasionally entertained Bryce-Jones and his charming wife in our executive box at Richington United. He is — was — a keen supporter and benefactor of the team. He will be sorely missed.'

'Where did they find his body, sir?' Williams was taking notes on his laptop.

'He was discovered early this morning in the executive washroom of the Bryce-Jones Investments Building on Canary Wharf. He had been murdered.'

'Isn't that a bit off our patch, sir? Surely that's a job for the City of London boys?'

'Don't waste time arguing, Inspector. The Commander has spoken with the Assistant Commissioner and he insists that we should take it on. Bryce-Jones was a Kings Richington man and it has been decided that my team will investigate the case.' He opened the folder he was carrying. 'The pathologist's initial report has been emailed to me. It appears that someone was waiting for him, hidden behind the door. As he went in, the killer grabbed his head and wrenched it backwards with such force that the violent jerk broke his neck.'

'Obviously someone who knew what they were doing and can kill using their bare hands,' observed Mitchell. 'Ex-military man possibly? SAS?' Mitch had done something of the sort before he joined the police.

Garwood ploughed on, anxious to tell Sir Barnaby that his team was on it and it would only be a matter of time before the killer was apprehended. 'His body was then positioned on the lavatory in a cubicle with the door shut. As it was Good Friday and there were few staff working, his body might well have remained there for some hours if his personal assistant hadn't realized he was missing and sent the cleaner in to bang on the door. The poor woman was severely traumatized.'

'But why would anyone want to kill a respectable family man?' asked Williams, tapping away.

'That's what you're being paid to find out, DC Williams.' Garwood turned to leave, then hesitated. 'There is just one more detail you need to know, and it's the main reason we are being asked to take this on.' He coughed, embarrassed. 'The city pathologist found blood and saliva round his mouth and down his lapel, inconsistent with the manner of death. It seems they found an item of — er — feminine hygiene forced down his gullet.'

'You mean a tampon, sir, like Wayne Jenkins?' Gemma was never one to beat about the bush.

'That's correct, DC Fox. Apart from that, the victims had nothing in common. They were from different backgrounds with contrasting lifestyles. The whole thing is bizarre. Well, get to it, you lot. The first twenty-four hours are crucial.' *And my next promotion could well depend on it*, Garwood thought.

* * *

The Commands of specialized homicide squads were split geographically. Once Garwood had gained command of his unit, he had taken pains to bring its success to the right people's attention. But for him, this job was only a springboard. The DCS was a career man, determined to rise to the top of his chosen profession. Garwood intended to become Assistant Commissioner. But one wrong move, one glimpse of him in a bad light in an important case, and his dream could be shattered. He had seen it happen to other senior policemen. It was not going to happen to him.

* * *

'What a way to die, sat on the khazi,' said Bugsy. 'No CCTV of course — inside or outside the bog.' He was writing what they knew on the board. There were photos of Toby Bryce-Jones with his wife and two children. Given the tampon connection with Wayne Jenkins, improbable though it seemed, they were comparing the two victims to try and establish any similarity that might help solve both murders. 'Give us what you've got on Bryce-Jones, Taffy.'

Williams consulted his laptop. 'Toby Bryce-Jones, aged thirty-nine. Ran his own investment company — online accounts show it's doing very well. Found wearing a designer suit and handmade shoes, with gleaming white teeth and well-groomed hair. Happily married with a massive country house in the expensive part of Kings Richington, down by the river, where he has a boat moored. Drove a top of the range BMW. Children, Ava and Chanelle, both at school in Cheltenham. Wife, Camilla, drives a Range Rover and works for a charity fundraising organization. Bryce-Jones was heavily insured but no reason to suspect his wife wanted him dead. No evidence of any extramarital hanky-panky. No obvious motive for his murder and certainly no reason why anyone would want to shove a tampon down his throat. Last known sighting was his secretary who saw him come in at nine o'clock on the morning he was killed, then he disappeared into the washroom and never came out.'

'OK, so how does that compare with our grimy friend Wayne?'

'Wayne Jenkins, aged forty, found wearing baggy jeans, dirty jacket, with stained teeth and lank, greasy hair. Lots of enemies and no moral compass. Erstwhile landlord of the Goat and Garter lived in a high-rise council flat down the grotty end of Lower Richington. Divorced with one son, Ronald, a plumber. There's a daughter, Tracy, a hairdresser, but she emigrated to New Zealand with her boyfriend a year ago. Ex-wife, Sandra, works as a cleaner and rides a bike. No insurance and every reason to suspect that his wife, and most other people who had dealings with him, might have wanted him dead. He'd certainly taken a few beatings over time. And of course, there's the drug pushing double-cross. But if that was the motive, why the tampon?'

'Why indeed?' Malone turned to PC Jackson. 'What about you, young Freud? You've got the psychology and criminology degree. Could these cases be linked in any way? Surely it's too much of a coincidence that a tampon should figure in two totally unrelated murder victims.'

Simon chewed his lip thoughtfully. 'I agree. On the face of it, these two victims couldn't be more dissimilar. But I don't believe we can explain the same modus operandi as just a ghastly coincidence. The idea behind victimology is to identify similarities between each of the victims, looking at age, lifestyle, hair and eye colour and whether they have met or worked together in the past or shared a common interest. These men are approximately the same age. Bryce-Jones was a successful, happily married businessman. Jenkins was a divorced petty criminal. It's very unlikely that they would have met or worked together in any capacity. I doubt if Bryce-Jones ever went into the Goat and Garter hoping to score some coke, nor would Jenkins have had any spare cash to speculate on the stock market. The only tenuous link is that they were both interested in football, Richington United in particular. The Chief Super told us he had entertained Mr and Mrs Bryce-Jones in his executive box and he was a keen supporter of the team. Jenkins had kept various memorabilia from his days as a young player. Given that everything else in his flat was shite, it was clearly important to him.'

DS Malone sighed. 'Ok, well, keep digging. We must be missing something, and we'll have Garwood in here soon, asking if we've arrested the killer yet.'

* * *

The team crawled over pretty well every aspect of the two men's lives. Little emerged that was new or helpful. Apart from the tampon connection, the only other detail that linked them was the timing of their murders. Each had been killed when the moon was full. It could be relevant or it could just be a coincidence.

Malone had asked Williams to get details of each man's financial situation. In cases of murder, his first instinct was to 'follow the money.' Jenkins's bank account varied hardly at all. Only his wages went in. He assumed that the money he made from his criminal activities was always paid in cash. He probably hid it, although Mitch and Simon hadn't found anything significant. But if he'd boasted about it when he was drunk, it might have been enough for someone to bump him off.

There was some interesting activity in Bryce-Jones's accounts. He checked it again, then called Bugsy over.

'I know Bryce-Jones ran a very successful investment company and he clearly knew what he was doing, but he seems to have had an extraordinary amount of luck.'

Bugsy looked over Aled's shoulder. 'I daresay there is a degree of luck in playing the stock exchange.'

'Hmm. Probably, but not this much. What do you know about insider trading?'

'Nothing, Taffy.'

'I know a bit about it from a friend of my dad's who works for one of the top investment trust providers. There are two kinds of insider trading — the legal kind is where insiders buy their own company's stock. Usually directors and managers or other employees. Then there's the illegal kind, where you gain a trading advantage through having access to confidential, non-public information. It could be about a new product, a merger with another company, a change in leadership or a fantastic earnings report about to be published. There's a fine line between the two and it's a bit blurred.'

'And you think Bryce-Jones was doing that?'

'Well, if you look at his accounts, he took some huge risks and they always paid off. I suppose that isn't sufficient for someone to want him dead . . .'

'Unless his illegal activity caused market shares to go tits up and someone lost a lot of loot, or even a whole company,' said Bugsy.

'I just think we shouldn't ignore the fact that he might not have been squeaky clean, despite what the Chief Super said.'

A sudden thought made Bugsy glance at the calendar. 'When's the next full moon?'

'Eighteenth of May,' Aled answered. 'I've already looked it up. Did you know that there are thirteen some years?'

'Lucky for some,' Bugsy answered. 'Did we ever interview the fragrant Camilla Bryce-Jones, guv?' he called.

'No,' said Jack. 'Garwood insisted on handling it himself. Said he didn't want an army of flat-footed coppers trampling on her sensitivities. I read his report of their conversation. Doesn't tell us anything. Full of words like "blameless" and "irreproachable." I think we should pay her a visit ourselves.'

'And after that, why don't we have a poke around his posh company offices in the city?' suggested Bugsy. 'Talk to some of his staff and examine the scene of the crime, in case the London boys have missed something.'

CHAPTER FOUR

The Bryce-Jones mansion was set in several acres of woodland. There were stables and paddocks with horses grazing. Ava and Chanelle were obviously keen on ponies, like most girls with wealthy parents. DI Dawes, DS Malone and DC Fox approached the house via a private lane to a gated drive, which swept past the fenced paddocks for around a quarter of a mile.

'Blimey,' said Bugsy. 'There's a few quid invested here. How would you like to inherit this from a dead husband, Gemma? And she had him insured for a packet.'

'I wouldn't, Sarge. What's the point of having kids, then farming them out to a posh school so you can fanny about with bits of charity work and hold ladies' luncheons? I bet she's got a massive kitchen she never cooks in, with one of those blooming great, expensive range cookers. My nan had a range. It belched out anthracite dust and gave her bronchitis. You couldn't even boil an egg on it without half an hour's notice.'

'I rather think Mrs Bryce-Jones will have something more modern than that,' said Jack. 'Let's see what she can tell us about her husband.'

The housekeeper let them into a spectacular reception hall with a full height ceiling and a carved oak staircase, leading up to a galleried landing. If they were expecting a weeping widow, they were mistaken. Camilla Bryce-Jones had it well held together. She swept down the stairs wearing an elegantly cut black dress with an emerald silk scarf thrown over one shoulder. *She won't have bought that in Primark, thought Gemma.* Camilla was the same age as Sandra Jenkins, although she looked a good ten years younger to Gemma. *That's what a privileged lifestyle does for you,* she thought. *Her outfit probably cost more than my whole wardrobe put together.*

Camilla indicated a door to their right. 'Please come into the drawing room. George Garwood phoned to tell me you were coming. Will you have some tea?'

They sat in a row, on a massive, brocade-covered sofa. Camilla sat opposite them in a matching armchair. The housekeeper brought in a teapot, and a Victoria sponge. Jack hoped Bugsy wouldn't get jam and cream on the upholstery. He lacked the coordination for fast food.

Dawes went through the usual condolences, then asked, 'Can you think of any reason why anyone would want to kill your husband, Mrs Bryce-Jones?'

'Absolutely not, Inspector. I've been over it again and again in my mind. He didn't have an enemy in the world. His employees loved him, he made generous donations to various charities and as I told George, it was his support for Richington United Football Team that enabled them to keep going.'

'Was football his favourite sport?' asked Malone.

'Well, I think he played a little when he was young. But nowadays, he just liked to go and watch. George and Cynthia Garwood have an executive box where Toby and I used to join them for dinner and watch the game. Not really my sort of thing, but it was a very pleasant way to spend an evening with friends.' She saddened. 'I miss him terribly. So do the girls. You will catch whoever killed him, won't you?'

They asked a few more questions but it soon became obvious to Jack that there was nothing more to be learned from Camilla Bryce-Jones. Bugsy and Gemma agreed that the woman was obviously telling the truth as she knew it.

'Maybe we'll have better luck with his investment company,' said Jack. 'We'll have a good look at the crime scene tomorrow.'

* * *

Jack and Bugsy needed a key to the executive washroom, which begged the question — how did the killer get in there? There was an overpowering reek of bleach that made their eyes smart.

'Smells like the cleaner has been back in here over the weekend with her mop,' gasped Jack. 'We won't find anything forensic that the original SOCOs didn't get.'

'Which was the square root of bugger all, according to the report they sent us,' Bugsy said.

'This killer certainly knows how to cover his tracks,' said Jack.

'Tell you what, guv. I think we should do a reconstruction of the crime. We know that the killer was waiting behind that door to pounce on Bryce-Jones when he came in. How did he know the next man to come in would be him? Did he go for a widdle at the same time every day? Then he breaks his neck, sticks a tampon down his throat and puts him on the bog in a cubicle. Now, Bryce-Jones wasn't fat, but he was tall — six foot something, like you, Jack. It can't have been easy to manoeuvre a dead weight from the door across to that cubicle at the far end, which was where he was found, and he didn't have a lot of time. I know it was Good Friday and there weren't many staff in, but someone else could have come in at any time.'

'I'm not even sure it's possible,' said Jack.

'Well, let's test it out. You be Bryce-Jones and I'll be the killer. You go out and come in again and I'll grab your head and wrench it back. But not hard, obviously.'

'Obviously.'

'And we'll time how long it takes from start to finish.'

Jack went out and immediately came back in. Bugsy had to reach up to grab his head because Jack was a good six inches taller. He gave it a brief tug.

'Now I'm disabled and you shove a tampon down my throat.'

Bugsy pulled a random bullseye from his pocket, popped it in Jack's mouth and counted to ten.

'Right, guv, now you're dead, so go all limp.'

Jack collapsed in a theatrical heap on the floor. 'OK, Bugsy, you've got to get me over there and into that cubicle.'

Bugsy lifted Jack under the arms. With a lot of puffing and panting, he managed to drag him across the floor and into the cubicle.

'Now I've got to sit you on the khazi.' That part was nigh on impossible. No amount of heaving was enough to lift a dead weight up onto the seat. Finally, Bugsy put both arms around Jack's waist and with a final mighty yank, managed to get him up on the lavatory, then he collapsed onto his knees, wheezing with the effort. At this point, the door opened and two Arab investors, wearing long, flowing white robes, wafted in. They took one look at Jack and Bugsy hastily emerging from the cubicle, turned and silently wafted back out.

'Perhaps we should have locked the door,' said Bugsy.

'That would have looked even worse.' Jack thought he might have split his trousers and he'd lost a button off his jacket. 'Let's go and talk to the staff. Employees are more likely to ditch the dirt on the boss after he's dead.'

'True. Could be something about Bryce-Jones's management style that would explain why someone wanted to rip his head off.'

But there wasn't. The male members of staff described him as a first-class boss, always ready to listen to new ideas and generous with bonuses when the market was good. When Jack hinted about insider trading, they were appalled. Nothing like that would have happened on Bryce-Jones's watch and they were shocked that such aspersions had been cast now that he was dead and couldn't defend his good name. The ladies, especially the young ones, were still inclined to reach for a tissue box at the mention of his name. He was 'such a lovely man.'

They solved the puzzle of how the killer obtained a key to unlock the washroom. There were several of them hanging up in the main office and executives just helped themselves. And his personal assistant confirmed that when Bryce-Jones came into the office at nine o'clock each morning, the first thing he did was go and wash his hands. He never wavered from this routine and everyone knew about it. It was only when he didn't return that she'd asked the cleaner to go in and see what had happened to him.

'Caroline, you say in your statement that you could see the door of the executive washroom at all times, which is how you knew that Mr Bryce-Jones hadn't come back out.'

'That's right, Inspector. He went in at approximately five past nine, after he asked me to get him some croissants. He never came back out.'

'Did you see anyone else go in there, before Mr Bryce-Jones?'

'No, nobody at all. And I was here from eight o'clock. I was the first person in the office. Nobody could have gone in there without me seeing them.'

'And you're absolutely sure nobody went in other than Mr Bryce-Jones?'

'Absolutely positive.' She hesitated. 'Well, only the cleaner. She popped in there after her night shift, just to make sure it was clean for when Mr Bryce-Jones got here.' Dawes and Malone looked at each other.

'Did you see her come out?' Dawes asked.

She concentrated hard. 'No, I don't believe I did, but I knew she'd gone because her trolley wasn't outside.'

'Do you think we might have a word with her?'

They found Hilda in the store cupboard where all the cleaning materials were kept. She looked at the duty lists.

31

'No, dear. I wasn't on the rota for that floor on Good Friday. I'd just finished my night shift on the second floor, and I was putting my stuff away when Caroline asked me to go in the washroom and find Mr Bryce-Jones. And very unpleasant it was, I don't mind telling you.'

'Can you tell us which cleaner was on the rota for that day?'

She looked at the lists. 'Nobody, dear. Management must have thought it wasn't necessary on account of it being Good Friday and there was hardly anybody working on that floor.'

* * *

On the way back to the station, Jack and Bugsy were trying to make sense of a nonsensical scenario.

'The killer arrives around eight-thirty, after Caroline has opened up. He's dressed like a cleaner.'

'That's a bit tricky, isn't it, Jack? Turning up in drag?'

'No, not really. You saw how Hilda was dressed. Black trousers, black polo shirt, trainers and a cap with the company logo that she leaves on her trolley.'

'Well, I think we can take it that he doesn't have any face fungus. Even if she wasn't watching too closely, I reckon Caroline might have noticed if Hilda had suddenly grown a beard and moustache.'

'He takes the cleaning trolley out of the cupboard and helps himself to a key to the washroom,' continued Jack. 'There's hardly anyone about because it's Easter. And anyway, nobody notices a cleaner coming and going in an office block, do they?'

'Then he goes into the washroom, locks the door, takes the key out, and waits behind it for Bryce-Jones to turn up,' Bugsy went on. 'Caroline has seen a cleaner go in, assumes it's Hilda and takes no notice.'

'Bryce-Jones arrives at nine o'clock, speaks to Caroline then goes in to wash his hands. The killer is waiting behind the door, breaks his neck, does the business with the tampon, then hides the body in a cubicle so that it won't be found immediately. Then he calmly goes back out, not caring if Caroline sees him or not — why would he? He puts the cleaning trolley away and goes home.'

'Bloody risky,' said Bugsy. 'Anything could have gone wrong. What if some random bloke from a different floor got caught short and nipped in there for a wee?'

'Calculated risk,' said Jack. 'We're dealing with a ruthless killer who is hell-bent on homicide and is prepared to take chances. What we don't know is who he is or why he's doing it.'

* * *

As soon as Jack got home, Corrie spotted his torn trousers and scuffed shoes.

'Have you been fighting in the playground again?'

He put his hands up. 'Please, Miss, Bugsy did it. We were reconstructing the Bryce-Jones murder and I was the dead body. It wasn't easy. Bugsy reckons he's put his back out.'

'I see, and what incredible breakthrough in modern murder detection did you achieve from this buffoonery, apart from ruining your trousers and losing a button?'

Jack had wondered that himself. 'We came to the conclusion that our serial killer's a very strong bloke dressed like a woman.'

CHAPTER FIVE

Cynthia Garwood poured herself a second hefty gin and tonic. She called to her husband, who was sitting at the dining table scanning the evening copy of the *Richington Echo* spread out in front of him.

'Do you want a drink, George?'

Garwood was anxious to see if his name was mentioned in the lurid and, in his view, over-sensationalized account of the two murders on the front page. The crime correspondent on the paper seemed to have it in for him and lost no chance to make him and his team look like incompetent idiots. He congratulated himself on having the sense to keep the business with that 'thing' in the victims' throats confidential. Thankfully, there was no mention of it in the article.

'Yes, I'll have a large scotch, please, no water.'

Cynthia poured the drink, handed it over and started to read over his shoulder.

'Very nasty.' She took a good swig of gin. 'Imagine having a tampon stuffed down your throat, then slowly suffocating as it swells up. You'd be surprised how much they expand, they come out at least twice the size than when you shove them—'

Garwood spluttered. 'Thank you, Cynthia, I really don't need to know the details.' He paused. 'How did you know they had tampons in their throats? I specifically ordered that the information should not be released to anyone outside the team. It could compromise the entire investigation. Who told you?'

She patted him on the head, comfortingly. 'All right, keep your wig on, Georgie. Marigold Catwater told me. She's Dr Hardacre's assistant. We go to the same Zumba class.'

'Are you telling me that all the women in the class know about it?' He started to go red in the face. 'This is appalling! What will Sir Barnaby think?'

'His wife's in the class too.'

* * *

Business was brisk at Coriander's Cuisine. She had orders stretching well into the summer, and Corrie's Kitchen was even busier. Cynthia Garwood entertained a lot and given that she'd struggle to cook beans on toast, she used Corrie's services a good deal and they had become friends. She had phoned to book a soirée supper for Saturday.

'You know, Corrie, you really need to get more exercise.'

Corrie smiled to herself. As if toiling over several hot stoves, supervising the staff and loading the vans for delivery wasn't enough exercise. This was obviously a less than subtle comment about Corrie's weight. She had to admit she was a bit on the chubby side. Well, a lot on the chubby side if she was being honest, but then, who trusts a skinny chef? Cynthia, of course, had a perfect figure, despite the amount of booze she put away.

'Why don't you come along to our Zumba class? All the girls go and it's the most super fun. Then afterwards, we escape to that new cocktail bar in Upper Richington to rehydrate with Prosecco.'

'OK, Cynthia, I'll try. When's the next one?'

'Six o'clock on May eighteenth.'

Corrie checked her business diary. She had a full staff working that day, so she thought she might give it a go. She just hoped she wouldn't strain something. She wasn't really the right shape for Zumba. 'Where is it?'

'Do you know Winston's Gym in Richington High Street? He teaches boxing to youngsters and trains some quite fit chaps, too. He lets us use the hall at the back and the showers afterwards.'

'Yes, I know it. See you there.'

* * *

Unlike Coriander's Cuisine, business was fairly slack with the Murder Investigation Team. Enquiries into the two murders were ongoing. In all truth, they were no further forward with finding the killer — if indeed it was only one killer. Chief Superintendent Garwood continued to dash in and out, on the hour, like a demented cuckoo in a clock, demanding results and telling them all to pull their fingers out.

Dead on nine o'clock, DI Dawes strode into the incident room carrying a strong Americano in a reusable mug. Bugsy was finishing the last of his breakfast — two sausage sandwiches from the canteen. Ketchup trickled down his chin and onto his tie.

'Anything new in, Bugsy?'

Bugsy shook his head. 'No, Jack. We thought we had another tampon murder, late last night. Bloke found dead with head injuries in an alley outside the pub. Witnesses said they heard him choking before he collapsed. Anyway, they dialled 999. Norman Parsloe arrived and did a fingertip pass to Big Ron and she poked about down his throat with her tweezers but there was no tampon, only a pickled onion. Then the landlord came forward. Turns out the bloke had drunk ten pints of Richington Ale, wolfed down a double ploughman's, then staggered outside to cycle home. He started to choke, then fell off his bike and bashed his head on the kerb.'

'I'm not sure if I'm sorry or relieved,' Jack remarked.

'That's what I said. The poor devil's dead, whichever way you look at it. He could at least have had the decency to get himself topped with a tampon and given us something to work on.'

'Yes, but if he'd had any decency, he wouldn't have drunk ten pints of Richington Ale.'

'True. Terrible stuff. Tastes like it's been filtered through one of my socks.'

* * *

'Sir, do we think there might be something significant in the fact that both tampon murders happened when there was a full moon?' PC Jackson wanted to know. 'I remember reading some research at uni that concluded there was no significant rise in violent crime related to the moon's phases. A more likely explanation is what's called the "illumination hypothesis." Criminals like enough light to see what they're doing but not so much as to increase their chance of getting nicked.'

Jack thought about that. 'Well, some folk do behave strangely at full moon, but then they're probably strange the rest of the time as well. Whether it would incite a bloke to kill, though, your guess is as good as mine. Yours is probably better than mine, given you've studied all this stuff.'

'What I want to know is, where does he get 'em from?' asked Malone.

'Get what, Bugsy?'

'Tampons. Does he go into Boots and buy a packet?'

'You can get them out of machines,' suggested DC Fox.

'Not in the gents you can't, Gemma. And if he goes in the ladies, I reckon someone would've noticed a bloke raiding the tampon machine.'

'In any event, I'll be very surprised if we get another tampon murder next full moon,' said Jack. 'Three murders would make this bloke a serial killer, and we've never had one of those in Kings Richington.' Jack crossed his fingers.

CHAPTER SIX

18 May. The Flower Moon

The Zumba class turned out to be more eventful than Corrie had expected. Pam, the instructor, was very striking. She wore dazzling yellow leggings and a pink glittery top with 'Zumba Goddess' emblazoned on the front. She shouted over the pumping music.

'Right, spread out everybody. I see we have some new ladies here tonight. Are there any health issues I should know about? Bad backs, funny turns, weak bladders? OK, let's go into our warm-up routine.' Pam turned the music up until it was deafening. 'Come on, ladies, give me some sweat! An hour's Zumba can burn off six hundred calories.' She leapt about, clapping and yelling. 'Forward with your right foot, back with your left, then bring your right foot up behind you and kick your bum.'

Corrie in her baggy T shirt and jogging pants felt like she'd stumbled into a dance class for the seriously bewildered. Thirty or so ladies of uncertain age and agility were hopping about the room, mostly at odds with the music. She did her best to keep up, but it was clearly a losing battle. Feeling in urgent need of hydration, she reached for her water bottle, but it was empty. She waved it at Cynthia, indicating that she was going out to the water cooler in the lobby. As she passed the gym, she could see boxers skipping, punching bags and sparring in the ring. It looked like Winston's business was doing well. She couldn't see him anywhere, but when she got outside, she found him sitting on a stool at the bar, with his head on his arms. She wondered if he was ill, so she went over.

'Hello, Mr Aduba. Are you OK?' He didn't answer, so she put her hand on his arm. Slowly, he lurched sideways and crumpled into a heap on the floor. His eyes were staring and there was blood and saliva around his mouth. Corrie didn't shock easily. She gasped a bit then felt for a pulse. There wasn't one. She was deciding whether to call Jack or an ambulance when there was a bloodcurdling scream from behind her. Cynthia Garwood had followed her out and was having a meltdown. She let out another ear-splitting shriek. Corrie shook her.

'Cynthia, stop screaming and sit down over there. Poor Mr Aduba has had a heart attack or something. I'm going to get my phone and call Jack.'

When Corrie's call came through at six-thirty, the team exchanged glances. It couldn't be murder, could it? Not another one. It would probably turn out to be natural causes. After all, boxing is a risky business. But it was 18 May and a full moon.

'OK, Bugsy, with me,' said Jack, pre-empting any specu-lation. 'We'll just go and make sure Corrie and Mrs Garwood are all right. I don't expect there'll be any need for an inves-tigation by the team.'

He was wrong.

* * *

An ambulance had been called, but although the paramed-ics had pronounced Aduba to be dead, they were unable to determine the cause of death and felt it might be suspicious, so they had called it in. The gym was empty by the time Dawes and Malone arrived. All the Zumba ladies had been sent home except for Corrie and Cynthia. Winston Aduba's body had been moved into the gym and was laid out on an exercise mat. The pathologist was already on the scene.

'Groundhog Day, Inspector Dawes?' Dr Hardacre clambered up from her ungainly squat over the corpse, displaying a good deal of sturdy knickered-leg in the process.

'Not natural causes, then, Doc?'

''Fraid not. I can't be sure exactly what happened to this poor man until I get him on the slab, but I can tell you he didn't die where he was found. He was propped up on that stool after he was killed.'

'Cause of death?' asked Jack, already suspecting the answer.

'Choked with a tampon.' Dr Hardacre held it up in her forceps. 'So far down his throat that I nearly couldn't get it. Post-mortem report as soon as I can.'

Chief Superintendent Garwood arrived to collect his wife, who was snivelling and demanding a large gin. He blustered about for a bit, asking why they were trampling all over the crime scene. 'Sort this out, Dawes. We need results and fast. Sir Barnaby's wife was in that exercise class. She may well be traumatized.'

'What about me?' yelped Cynthia. 'Don't you care if I've been traumatized?'

'Come along, Cynthia. Stop making a fuss.' He hustled her out to the car.

* * *

Back home, Jack poured two stiff cognacs. Corrie took a good swig and gasped as the heat engulfed her throat.

'You didn't ask if I was traumatized.'

'Didn't need to,' said Jack. 'I know you're made of sterner stuff. Besides, the number of times you've interfered in my murder cases, there's very little gruesome nastiness that you haven't already seen.'

'I don't interfere, darling. I just offer assistance where I can.' She took another gulp. 'Poor Mr Aduba. He'll be missed. He's helped a lot of wayward young men in Kings Richington. He channelled their street aggression into boxing.'

'Unlike football, which you say creates aggression,' teased Jack.

'Precisely. But Winston Aduba used to be a footballer too. He played for Richington United as centre half. He had to give it up after an injury, so he turned to boxing instead.'

'That's interesting,' said Jack. 'You're very well informed. How did you know that?'

'His brother's wife, Florence, works for Corrie's Kitchen. You see, my local knowledge, that you choose to call gossip, can be a great help. What shall we have for supper?'

* * *

The post-mortem report on Winston Aduba stated that he had received a direct blow, most probably with the knife edge of the killer's hand, to the nerve that branches off to the spinal cord, close to his kidneys. That in itself can cause death, but in this instance it did not. Like the other two victims, Aduba had choked to death on a tampon while still alive.

There was a tense atmosphere of disbelief around the table in the incident room. Jack sat down at one end. The troops needed some reassurance.

'Right, folks. Let's do some brainstorming. We're looking at three murders in three months and they were all Kings Richington men.' The room was silent for a few moments, everyone waiting for someone to say what they were all thinking. 'And anyone who mentions Midsomer has to buy the cakes for a month.' This broke the tension. 'In view of the bizarre cause of death, I think we're safe to assume the murders were committed by the same killer. Three murders, so we have a serial killer and we need to stop him before there's a fourth. Now we have a third victim, let's have another go at identifying any similarities. DS Malone will write them down on the whiteboard.'

They shouted suggestions.

'They were all aged around forty,' offered Aled.

'They all had a past connection to Richington United football team,' said Gemma.

'They were all killed when there was a full moon.' Simon still believed it might be significant.

'They were all disabled by expert blows from someone who knew what he was doing.' Mitch's ex-military experience told him this killer was trained.

'Sir, shouldn't we acknowledge the differences as well as the similarities?' Aled consulted his laptop. 'Jenkins was a petty criminal, fat, dirty, divorced, no friends, no car, lived in a scuzzy flat and got beaten up regularly. Bryce-Jones was well-educated, ran his own company in London, posh house in the best part of Kings Richington, wife's a fundraiser, kids in private school and he drove a BMW. Aduba taught boxing to tearaways, ran a fight club with money prizes, happily married with four kids, drove a battered Volkswagen.'

'Good point. So how and why were these men selected by the killer? And more to the point, how can we get a heads up on who might be next?'

'Sir, might there be a connection between the full moon and the murder weapon? Tampons are linked to the menstrual cycle which happens around every lunar month.'

The team jeered. 'Leave off, Gemma. What's that got to with anything? Are you saying this bloke kills because he's having his "time of the month?"' There was general laughter.

'No, that's a valid point, Gemma,' said Jack. 'We shouldn't discount it.'

They continued until the board was full of scribbled notes surrounding the macabre forensic shots of the three victims, faces blue and cyanosed from choking. It was three months since the first tampon murder and as far as Jack could see, they were no closer to catching the killer.

CHAPTER SEVEN

When Corrie arrived at Corrie's Kitchen next morning, there was a sympathetic huddle around Florence Aduba. Corrie went to offer her condolences.

'I'm so sorry about your brother-in-law, Florence. Your husband must be devastated to have lost his brother, never mind Winston's family.'

Florence nodded. 'Errol and Winston were very close. They ran the boxing gym together. I don't know what Errol will do now he's got to manage on his own.' She paused. 'They say it was you who found Winston's body, Mrs Dawes. What do you think happened to him?'

News travels fast, thought Corrie — especially bad news. She hadn't been a copper's wife all these years without learning that you didn't give away any information that wasn't already out there.

'I really don't know, Florence, but I know that the police are conducting a thorough enquiry to find out.'

Florence lowered her voice. 'Winston was murdered, wasn't he? Errol was worried something like this might happen.'

Corrie lowered her voice, too. 'Really? Why was that?'

'Winston used to promote some quite important fights with promising young boxers. It was all legal — licence and doctor on hand and everything. But what wasn't legal was the betting. Often very large sums of money.'

'Yes, but I expect that happens quite a lot in boxing, legal or not. It wouldn't be a reason for someone to kill him, would it?'

Florence hesitated. 'No, but fixing fights for money might be.'

Corrie chewed her lip. 'Is that what Winston was doing?'

'That's what Errol told me. I was worried that he'd be drawn into it. Then Winston took a large amount of cash from one of the London promoters to get our man to throw a fight. Big names betted but when the time came, their man was ring rusty — hadn't had a decent fight in months. So our man wouldn't take a dive and he won the fight. Some important men in the fight game lost a lot of money. They were very angry, according to Errol. He believes they killed Winston as a punishment. Oh, Mrs Dawes, I'm so worried. You don't think they'll come after Errol, do you?'

Blimey, thought Corrie. *They just might.* 'Don't worry, Florence, I'll pass this information on to the police. They may want to talk to Errol.'

* * *

When Jack got home that evening, Corrie was waiting for him with her news.

'I've got some information for you about Winston Aduba,' she said. 'It's important.'

'Right. What's for dinner?'

'Cottage pie. It was left over from the Corrie's Kitchen orders.'

'Good, I like cottage pie. Can we have brown sauce?'

'Jack, I wish you would concentrate. It's like talking to a toddler. Florence Aduba told me today that Winston had been fixing fights for money. Which was OK while none

44

of the gangsters were involved. But then there was this big fight, with lots of money on it, and the gangsters all bet really heavily. Winston took a wad to ensure our man took a dive. But the other guy was rubbish and had a rusty ring or something. Anyway, our man punched his lights out in the third.'

'Corrie, you are developing a very lurid turn of phrase. Besides which, this is dangerous territory. I wish you wouldn't interfere. Those sorts of men wouldn't hesitate to harm you if they thought you were involved.'

'I didn't have a choice, Jack. Poor Florence is scared that they killed Winston and now they're coming back for Errol. I said you'd sort it all out.'

'Of course you did, darling. Thanks for that. Bugsy and I will go and see Errol in the morning.'

* * *

They found Errol Aduba in the empty gym. Jack noticed that there was CCTV outside the main door and in the gym, but not in the bar. At least they'd be able to see everyone who came in. A notice on the door said, 'Closed due to family bereavement.' As Dawes and Malone pushed through the swing doors, Errol jumped violently, clearly on edge. After the customary expressions of condolence, Dawes asked Errol who would have been the last person to see Winston alive.

He thought for a bit. 'That would've been me, if you don't count the bastard who killed him. I saw him go into the bar to get a bottle of water.'

'I'm sorry to ask this, but have you any idea who might want to harm your brother?'

He hesitated. 'Er . . . no. Winston was a good bloke. He never 'ad no enemies.'

'So you can't think of any reason for his murder? Only, your wife mentioned that Winston had taken money to fix a fight, it had gone badly wrong and some London racketeers had lost heavily.'

Aduba cast a weary hand over his eyes and sighed. 'Flo shouldn't have said nothing.'

'She's worried about you, Errol. She's afraid you're implicated and they might come after you next.'

Clearly that thought had crossed Errol's mind, too. 'No, I never 'ad nothing to do with that side of the game. I just trained the lads, kept 'em fit and did some sparring. Winston took care of the match arrangements. He couldn't do much of the ring work on account of 'is broken ankle. Did it years ago, playing football.' He paused, then decided to tell the two coppers everything. Winston was dead — no point in hiding anything. He had a wife and kids to consider, never mind Winston's wife and kids. 'It's true, Winston took a hefty bung on the last tournament. Our lad was supposed to take a dive in the fifth, but his opponent was rubbish — overweight, ring rusty and hardly landed a decent punch. If our lad had thrown the fight, it would've looked obvious, so he put him down in the third. Lovely combination of a left jab to the body, followed by a straight right then a left hook.' Errol was dancing about, shadow boxing by way of a demonstration. 'Put 'is lights out proper. He never even saw the knockout punch coming.'

Bugsy was dodging the flying fists, fearing the same might happen to him. 'Do you know who the promoter was that gave Winston the bribe?'

'No, mate, I don't. And I don't want to know, neither. I kept right out of it.'

Further questions didn't provide any more information than what they already had. Malone warned Errol that if anyone contacted him, asking for the money to be returned, he should call the police straight away.

He grimaced. 'Too bloody right I will.'

They took away Winston's laptop, some documents they found in his tiny office and the CCTV footage from around the time he was killed. These were handed over to Clive and his techies in the MIT team with little expectation that they would help identify his killer. The London boys were too smart to leave a trail. And if it was a punishment killing, where did the tampon come in?

* * *

DC Mitchell and DC Fox went to see Ella Aduba, Winston's widow. She lived in a terraced house in the back street behind the gym. Ella's mother, Lena, was with her, helping look after the four children, who were very close in age. The noise was deafening, with each child demanding attention. Gemma guessed that the eldest couldn't have been more than five. He kept pulling at his mother's skirt and shouting. The youngest was just a baby, wrapped in a shawl in its grandmother's arms and screaming the place down. Two little girls were on the floor, pulling each other's hair and shrieking. Again, Gemma was making the inevitable comparisons between Sandra Jenkins, Camilla Bryce-Jones and now Ella Aduba. It was an interesting exercise in social stratification but more importantly, it accentuated the diversity of the victims' lives. They had to have something in common that would give MIT the motive for the killings, though it was proving difficult to see what it could be.

'Mrs Aduba, can you tell us anything about your husband's death? Anything that might help us to catch the killer?' DC Mitchell doubted it. The poor woman was distraught.

'Killer?' she sobbed. 'What killer? Winston wasn't killed. He died of a brain haemorrhage due to boxing. Errol told me. Why are you saying he was killed?'

Oh bugger, thought Mitch. No one has told her that her husband was murdered. How could that be? On second thoughts, she probably hadn't been out of the house or seen any television news with all those kids to look after. If uniform had done what was known as "the death message" to notify her of her husband's death, they wouldn't have gone into detail but left it to the detectives. On the other hand, maybe they did tell her but she hadn't heard, due to the racket the kids were making.

'I'm afraid your husband was murdered,' said Gemma. 'I'm so sorry.'

Ella began screaming as well, then, which frightened the children and increased the volume. Before they left, Gemma tried to tell her that the police would appoint a family liaison officer to help her, but it was impossible to know if she had understood.

Lena caught up with them on their way out. She was still holding the baby, who had mercifully stopped screaming but was still very red in the face.

'The police told me that Winston had been murdered but I didn't tell Ella. She was in a bad enough state without that. Errol thinks some London gangsters did it. Is that what the police think? Will these men come after Ella for money?'

'I'm afraid we can't discuss that,' said Mitch, 'but I can tell you that the police are following several lines of enquiry. We will catch who did this, I promise.'

Fat chance, thought Gemma. At the moment, they were pissing in the wind.

Mitch walked to the car with a handkerchief over his nose. 'What was that awful stink? Do you suppose there's something wrong with the drains? Maybe we should get the council in to investigate.'

Gemma grinned. 'No need. It was the baby.'

* * *

'Right, guv, so all three blokes had skeletons in their cupboards.' Bugsy bit into a jumbo sausage roll. He couldn't think properly when he was hungry. He claimed it was low blood sugar and he needed to eat vast quantities of junk food throughout the day or there was a risk he'd faint. The pockets of his scruffy jacket invariably contained a half-eaten sandwich, bits of pork pie and a bar of chocolate, covered in fluff.

Jack tolerated the endless trails of crumbs and ketchup because when Bugsy was fuelled up, there was none better than him. If Poirot's "little grey cells" depended on fish, then Bugsy's relied on pies, chips and pizza.

DS Malone had been Jack's anchor-man for more years than he cared to remember. Jack valued his honesty, probity and loyalty. Also, he was a good man to have at your side if the going got rough. He had never sought promotion beyond Detective Sergeant, regarding top brass as 'a bunch of shiny-arsed uniform carriers who sit at a desk all day totting up overtime claims,' but he had the deepest respect for DI Dawes and would have followed him into Hades.

'I reckon we all have skeletons, when you come right down to it,' said Jack. 'What are you thinking?'

'Well, maybe we're looking for a bloke who bought some moody coke from Jenkins, lost money on Bryce-Jones's insider trading, then backed the wrong boxer at one of Aduba's fixed fights.'

'If that's true, our serial killer leads a very colourful life,' observed Jack. 'And he doesn't have a lot of luck, either.'

* * *

When they got back to the station, PC Simon Jackson was hovering, waiting to speak to them.

'What can we do for you, young Freud? Or should I say Jung-Freud.' Bugsy chuckled at his own joke. Simon gave him a watery smile. Bugsy was totally un-PC with everyone but never offensive, so the team accepted him as such.

'What have you got, Simon?' Jack was aware that this young copper had the brains and the determination to go far in the service and fast. He had resolved to give him all the support he could. He could be a Chief Constable in the not so distant future and, as Corrie would say, 'It never hurts to keep your bouillabaisse on a backburner in case the French invade.'

'I've been thinking, sir. You mentioned we need to get a heads up on who might be the killer's next victim.'

'Well, I'm rather hoping there won't be another victim, but what did you have in mind?'

'Profiling, sir. Criminal profiling functions on the principle that every serial killer works to a certain set of values, a sort of signature. Once you identify the signature, you can use it to make a positive identification of your murderer.' Simon was in his stride now, keen to use his psychology to good effect. 'Then there's victimology. You study the similarities between each of the victims in order to identify a definite pattern in the killer's approach. We've applied some of this already — victimology looks at age, lifestyle, whether they've met or worked together in the past or shared a common interest. This intelligence can be used by a profiler to build up a picture of the killer and predict his next move, hopefully before he can strike again.'

'And are you proposing to do this criminal profiling yourself?'

Simon looked shocked. 'No, sir. It needs an expert, a professional with proven expertise. We'd need to bring someone in.'

'That's all very well on television, son,' said Malone, 'but I'm not sure it'll work in real policing. And I can't see the Chief Super being impressed, especially if he has to fork out from the area budget. What do you think he'll say, Jack?'

'I know exactly what he'll say, but it's worth a try.'

* * *

'Psychobabble!' asserted Garwood. 'A load of pseudoscientific nonsense and half-baked ideas. What's wrong with common sense, sound judgement and good, old-fashioned police work?'

'Nothing, sir, but it isn't getting us very far at the moment.'

'Well, work harder, man! There must be other lines of enquiry you haven't followed up yet. The smart money says all three murders were perpetrated by the same man. He must have left some clues behind to give himself away. Find them, Dawes, find them!'

Jack thought the old man might have a point, so he and the team spent several days going through all the reports

50

from the Scenes of Crime Officers, uniform officers, witness statements, photographs and anything else that might prove relevant. The conclusion was that this killer, whoever he was, had covered his tracks impeccably. No fingerprints or DNA, no clumsy evidence left behind, such as the tampon applicator — nothing. According to Dr Hardacre, no weapon was used in any of the three cases. The killer had disabled his victims using his bare (gloved) hands. Each of the tampons had been carefully dissected in the laboratory and subjected to every possible test, but the only DNA on them belonged to the victim.

CHAPTER EIGHT

17 June. The Strawberry Moon

As the next full moon approached, in the early hours of 17 June, there was an air of anticipation among the MIT. The following day, every time the phone rang, at least three people jumped up to answer it. Uniform had been briefed that anything remotely suspicious should be passed straight through. Even Garwood was jumpy and kept asking for an update. It was late in the evening when Dawes called a halt.

'OK, troops, time to call it a day. I think if another poor sod had been killed, we'd have heard about it by now. The sick bastard has obviously reached his quota. Time to go up the pub.'

The tension lifted and they chatted and laughed as they put on coats and trooped out.

Jack bought the first round. The team had been working long hours with total dedication.

'Do you really think our killer has stopped, sir?' asked Aled.

'It looks like it, but we still have to catch him. He's ended three lives. We can't let up until we have him.'

* * *

Corrie was stirring something in a cast iron skillet on the stove when Jack got home. The aroma was appetizing and Jack realized how hungry he was. He went and stood beside her. 'That smells good, sweetheart.' He picked up a spoon. 'Can I taste?'

She giggled. 'You can if you like, but it's horse laxative in a bran mash. The little girl next door has a pony with colic. Your dinner is in the oven. Not that you deserve it, as I can smell that you've been in the pub for the last couple of hours.'

'Sorry, darling, but it was such a relief finding out we'd got past the full moon without another murder. The team needed to relax. Bugsy was relaxed as a newt.'

'Is the serial killer thing all over now, then?'

'Well, not really. We still have three unsolved murders that can't be ignored and families who need answers. And as Garwood keeps reminding me, it doesn't look good on the team's clear-up rate. But I confess, I seriously suspected there'd be another last night. Successful serial killers get over-confident and don't usually stop until they're caught. I'm glad I was wrong.'

'Yes, of course. The whole thing has been ghastly, especially for their loved ones. How do you fancy salmon en croute with a cheeky little Chablis?'

* * *

Next morning, the edgy atmosphere of the previous day had lifted and the team carried on with their work as usual. It wasn't to last for long. Bugsy had just bitten into a Chelsea bun the size of a small cushion, when the door was flung open and Garwood strode in. His face was like thunder. The room went instantly chilly.

'Inspector Dawes, may I have a word? On second thoughts, you had all better hear this.' They gathered round in silence. 'I have just been at a meeting with Sir Barnaby, who has had a call from the Chief Constable of Northumbria Police. On the morning of 17 June on the Fish Quay in

North Shields, a fishmonger by the name of Joe Roberts was found dead on his slab, surrounded by raw fish.'

'That's sad, sir, but what's it got to do with us?' Jack asked.

'The reason the Chief Constable contacted the London Metropolitan Police, Inspector, was because Roberts didn't die of natural causes. He was choked by a tampon that the killer had rammed down his throat.'

There were several sharp intakes of breath. The predominant feeling was one of disbelief. The Chief Superintendent continued, 'It appears our serial killer hasn't stopped, simply moved on. As you are aware, the details of our three cases are on the police database and Northumbria Police identified the similarities in the modus operandi. Rather than duplicate existing efforts, I have been requested to send a small team of officers to North Shields to investigate. Dawes, I shall leave you to arrange this, but I should like you to lead the team. Thank you, that is all.' He strode out.

'Well, what do you make of that, guv?' Bugsy was uncharacteristically sombre. 'Why would our man travel nearly three hundred miles to commit another murder? It's got to be significant, if only we could find out what connects them all.'

'We need to get up there and have a look. I'll take you, with DC Williams and DC Fox. While we're gone, PC Jackson, I'd like you to have a look at what's needed to bring in a criminal profiler. Even the Chief Superintendent will have to agree that we need some expert advice if we're ever going to stop this maniac.'

* * *

'How long will you be away?' asked Corrie. Jack had come home and announced he was off to the North East first thing in the morning.

'I've no idea, darling. Look, you don't have to pack for me. I'm sure I can manage.'

'Yes, I do. Otherwise you'll get there to find you have ten shirts and no knickers. I can't believe there's been another tampon murder. It's gross. And why North Shields?'

'That's what we're going to find out.'

'Northumberland isn't very big, is it?' remarked Corrie.

'Oh, just about the same size as Luxembourg, I believe.'

'Maybe next time, the killer will murder someone in Barbados, then I could come with you.'

'That, if I may say so, is a very self-seeking and callous notion. We should be so lucky.'

* * *

They caught the train from London Kings Cross at eight forty-five. It was due to arrive in Newcastle around twelve-fifteen. Northumbria police had arranged for them to be met by Detective Sergeant Billy Purvis, who would drive them to Northumbria Police HQ.

Bugsy's experience of the North was that it was always bloody cold, even in June, so he'd packed every sweater he possessed and was wearing a hefty overcoat. When they got off the train, he waited for a blast of cold air to greet them, but it was, instead, baking hot.

DS Purvis was holding up a board with 'DI Dawes' scrawled on it in felt pen.

'Welcome to Newcastle, gentlemen.' He said it with the accent on 'castle.' 'My instructions are to take you to your hotel to drop off your luggage and then to headquarters, if that's OK with you, Inspector.'

'That's fine,' said Dawes. 'This is DS Malone, DC Williams and DC Fox. They are fully up to speed with the details of the cases. The sooner we make a start, the better.'

Bugsy's stomach growled audibly. 'Any chance of some lunch first? Young Taffy's stomach thinks his throat's been cut.'

'Oh aye,' said Purvis. 'There's some cracking fish and chip shops doon Tynemouth.'

They piled into the car, and soon they were following the coast road towards Longsands beach, a mile of golden sand where folk were sunbathing and surfing. Bugsy realized he'd brought entirely the wrong gear and he'd have to find a shop to buy some short-sleeved shirts. He'd had a somewhat jaundiced view of 'the North' but now decided that some of it wasn't half bad. As they rounded King Edward's Bay, he spotted a fish shack with a board that declared it served 'fabulous fish, locally caught, simply served.' He pointed. 'That'll do me, Billy.'

While they were eating, Jack asked, 'What can you tell me about Joe Roberts, Sergeant?'

'He was a fishmonger, doon the Fish Quay. Forty-one years old, unmarried. Only relative, his dad. No form, well, nothing official on the police computer, anyway. No known enemies. But someone didn't like him. We found him dead on his marble slab, among the wet fish.'

'When you say, "no form, nothing official on the police computer," I sense you suspected him of something, but couldn't make it stick.' Jack was good at detecting an undercurrent.

'Aye, sir. Nothing major, like. But the word was he used to buy cheap fish from boats who'd overfished their quota, then sell it from his shop next day. It must have happened during the neet, because we never caught them at it. Somebody could have objected.'

'Yeah, but not enough to kill him, surely?' said Bugsy. 'Bad business, poor bugger.' He resisted the urge to call it a 'fishy business.' He wasn't at home now, and some people might misunderstand his gallows humour.

'When was he found?' asked DC Williams, who had his notebook out and was writing things down.

'Early on the morning of June seventeenth.'

After the moon had been in full phase at 4:31 am, thought Aled. He had recorded all the phases of the moon on his laptop.

'He was always doon on the quay early, to buy legal fish from the trawlers. When he didn't turn up, his father gan doon to look for him.'

'Who would have had the last known sighting?' asked Malone.

'His last customer before he closed up the neet afore, like.'

'Where is this Fish Quay? We'll need to take a look at the crime scene at some point.'

'As it goes, sir, we're not far from it. If we carry on doon the coast, through Tynemouth Village, we'll come to the Fish Quay on the way to your hotel at Royal Quays.'

CHAPTER NINE

Joe Roberts's shop had police tape all around it, and the police had pulled the blinds over the windows to stop the more ghoulish members of the public from peering in. Three days on, it stank of rotting fish, as nobody had thought to get rid of them, even after Roberts's corpse had been taken off to the mortuary. As DC Fox pointed out, if the deceased had a dog or cat, even a budgie, you called the RSPCA to come and get it. Nobody would take responsibility for re-homing Roberts's live crabs and lobsters. She was half inclined to take the rubber bands off their claws and chuck them back in the sea.

'Here's where his father found him, sir.' DS Purvis indicated the white slab that ran the length of the shop front.

Bugsy spotted the CCTV camera outside the shop. 'Can we take a look at what that camera recorded, Billy? We might be able to see who Joe's last customer was.'

'Sorry, no. We didn't find any recordings. Our lads took the camera doon to see why, and the wires had corroded in the salt air. Doubt if it's been tested since Joe took over the business from his father.'

'Have you had the pathology report yet?' asked Jack.

'Aye, sir. It was the findings of the post-mortem that prompted the boss to ask for your help. Propa nasty, an' all.'

'Can we go the mortuary, next, Sergeant? I think it would be useful to take a look at our victim before we go to your incident room at HQ.'

* * *

One mortuary is very like another and this one was no different from the one back home, except that it was presided over by Doctor Geordie Armstrong rather than 'Big Ron' Hardacre. As his name suggested, Doctor Armstrong spoke broad Geordie, and at one stage, Bugsy wondered if he was doing it on purpose to make life difficult for the London cops.

'You've set the time of death between one and five o'clock in the morning, Doctor.' Dawes was thumbing through the report prior to studying it properly when they reached the incident room.

'Aye. Could be that. Divvent pin us doon. The body was on a marble slab owa neet, covered in ice and fish. There's a canny margin, like.'

'Sorry?' said Dawes, politely.

'I think what Doc Armstrong means,' translated DS Purvis, 'is that the effect of the ice around the body could skew the time of death.'

'Aye, wisn't a just sayen that, man, Billy?'

'Cause of death, Doctor?' ventured Malone.

The report said the killer pulled his arms straight back — there was considerable bruising — then drop-kicked his spine, almost severing it. Boot prints indicated that the damage was inflicted by heavy-duty work boots. But Roberts didn't die instantly. He would have lain paralysed for some time, unable to move or scream, while he slowly choked to death on the tampon rammed down his throat. The killer's trademark.

59

'Hoy that specimen dish owa here, man, Billy.' DS Purvis passed it over and Doc Armstrong held it out. 'He-yor, Inspector.' Soaked in blood and mightily swollen was the trademark in question.

'Not your everyday murder weapon, Doctor.'

'Nah. Canny idea though but.'

* * *

When they arrived at Northumbria HQ, Inspector Dawes was taken through to top brass. The Chief Superintendent thanked him for coming.

'Your Chief Superintendent Garwood tells us you've had three murders with a similar MO.'

'That's right, sir.'

'Well, let's hope that, together, our teams can combine intelligence and solve these gruesome murders. If you need anything, just let my lads know. Carry on, Inspector, and good luck.'

'We're going to need it, sir,' said Dawes. 'We've had precious little luck so far.' But the key to the whole investigation, an elusive MacGuffin that would eventually lead to the killer's downfall, was about to fall into his hands.

* * *

The Northumbria incident room was very well-structured, with all the relevant information clearly set out on the white-board in methodical order. Jack's team was welcomed with tea and doughnuts. He couldn't help thinking that his incident room back home would appear chaotic in comparison. But it was how they worked best, so he never complained. Jack and Aled were adding what they knew in terms of modus oper-andi, trying to build a picture that would assist both teams. Like the MIT, the inspector running the investigation had found no motive for the fishmonger's murder, despite a thor-ough trawl through his house and lifestyle, both of which were mundane and uninteresting. And as for the murder weapon, he declared that in thirty years of policing, he'd never seen anything like it and sincerely hoped he never would again.

Bugsy had just finished his second doughnut when Gemma Fox spotted it. On a table in the corner of the room were a number of random items of interest collected from Joe Roberts's house. She had been carefully sifting through them. Even though she'd been told that they'd been checked and there was nothing significant amongst them, it didn't hurt to look with a fresh pair of eyes.

She gestured to Malone. 'Sarge, come and look at this. I think this is what we've been searching for — the link between our four victims.'

She pointed to a photograph in a frame, carefully protected by a transparent evidence bag. Bugsy looked, then called across to DI Dawes. 'Inspector, there's something here I think you should see.'

Jack came across to the table. 'Sergeant, you're getting jam and sugar all over the exhibits. Try not to leave a trail of food behind like you do at home.'

'Sorry, guv, but look at this. Gemma spotted it.'

Jack looked. Then he picked it up and peered more closely at it. Then he called to DS Purvis. 'Billy, where did this photograph come from?'

Purvis looked. 'The victim's father gave it to us. It was on his mantelpiece. He thought it might be useful, but we couldn't see how. Didn't want to upset the old man, he was distraught enough as it was.'

'Do you think we might take it out of the frame?'

'Aye, if you think it's helpful, sir. It wasn't anywhere near the crime scene.'

They took it out of the bag and carefully cut around the backing paper. Bugsy slid the yellowing photograph out from behind the glass, turned it over and cursed.

'Christ on a bike! You see what this could mean, guv?'

'Yes, Bugsy, I think I do. I think we all do.' Gemma nodded in agreement and swiftly took photographs of both sides with her phone. Jack passed it to DS Purvis. 'Billy, could you let me have a photocopy of this — both sides, please? Then scan it and send it to my team in Kings Richington? Thanks.'

* * *

DC Williams caught the train back to London. He messaged the team to explain the relevance of the photograph and said he'd fill in any gaps when he arrived. They should start moving on with enquiries. Jack, Bugsy and Gemma stayed on to interview Bert Roberts, Joe's father. After the initial expressions of sympathy — the man was clearly shattered at the death of his son — Bugsy produced the photograph.

'Bert . . . may I call you Bert? I believe this photo was on your mantelpiece and you kindly lent it to the police to assist with their enquiries. It looks like a photo of a football team. Can you identify any of the young men in it?'

Bert Roberts smiled sadly and jabbed a finger at it. 'Aye, that's my son, Joe, sitting in the middle at the front. He was the goalie and a bloody fine one too, young as he was. Hardly ever let one through.'

'When was this photograph taken, Bert?' Jack asked gently.

'Must be over twenty years ago now.' He turned the photo over and pointed to the writing. 'See? Richington United Under-21s. They're all in the picture. Some of their names are on the back and what position they played. Team photo it were. Course, I don't remember them now, but they were good lads. Trained hard and got good results. Some of them went on to play for professional teams. Our Joe got a job with Newcastle United. It's why we left the South and came up here.'

'Do you know if he was still in contact with any of the other players?'

'Not that I knew about. He broke his leg, see. Nasty tackle when he was going for a save. After that, he couldn't play anymore. That's when the wife and I bought the fish shop. She passed on three years ago, I retired and Joe took over. Now he's gone, I don't know what I'll do with it.'

There were tears in Bert Roberts's eyes. Jack thought they'd troubled him enough. And he'd certainly provided them with some valuable information.

* * *

On the train going back, Bugsy was examining the names on the back of the photo.

'There they are, guv. Wayne Jenkins, striker and captain. Toby Bryce-Jones, left back. Winston Aduba, central defender and now Joe Roberts, goalkeeper. There are eleven of them in the team, plus some reserves and the coach. You don't think this nutter plans to knock 'em all off one at a time, do you?'

'Well, if he does, we need to stop him before he can. But what's the motive?'

'Maybe he didn't make the first team,' suggested Gemma. 'Maybe he got a bad injury that crippled him. Maybe he was a referee and they were nasty to him and called him rude names.'

'I doubt it, given the strength it would need to disable these guys. And bear in mind, this photo was taken twenty years ago. Nobody bears a grudge that long, do they? Why now? What's triggered this killing binge?' Jack was puzzled.

'And where does the tampon fit in?' asked Bugsy. 'No, don't answer that.'

'Now we've got a possible fix on how the victims are selected,' said Jack, 'we have to figure out the significance of the full moon and the tampons. And if PC Jackson has found us a criminal profiler, hopefully he'll be able to do that.'

CHAPTER TEN

'If the killer is sticking to his insane lunar timetable, we have until sixteenth July to catch him before he kills again. That's only a couple of weeks away.'

Inspector Dawes was back in the incident room at Richington Station, where the team had added the new information to the whiteboard, together with an enlarged copy of the football team photograph.

'Actually, sir, I don't think he's insane,' offered PC Jackson. 'At least, he is, obviously, but not in the way we might think.'

'How many ways are there to be crackers, son?' asked Bugsy.

'Quite a few actually, Sarge. Especially if the crime is murder.' Simon was getting into his stride. 'It's well-documented that most serial killers have a desire to experience an emotional or sexual release as the result of inflicting pain and death on others.'

'Nice,' said Bugsy. 'So how would we recognize this gentleman if we met him in the street?'

'Most probably, you wouldn't. Psychotics devolve from what is mostly a lucid state of mind into a pathological state of frenzy, resulting in murder. What triggers it depends on their own particular hang-up.'

'You know, Simon, that's pretty scary,' said Mitch. 'It means that most of the time, the killer would appear normal, so everybody's off guard.'

'Exactly. A criminal profiler would study all the information we have and attempt to build up an accurate picture of the killer.'

'Fine, Simon,' agreed Jack. 'So where do we find such a man?'

'Professor Davenport, sir. A lecturer at my uni and the best in the business.'

'OK, I'll square it with Chief Superintendent Garwood.'

* * *

Garwood was surprisingly acquiescent about bringing in a profiler.

'OK, Dawes, go ahead. This is what modern policing is all about and we must use all the resources at our disposal. Get this professor on board and keep me informed.'

In fact, the reason Garwood had changed his mind about 'psychobabble was because the Commander had threatened to stand him down and draft in another Chief Superintendent as SIO if he didn't get results soon. The *Richington Echo* was having a field day with inflammatory headlines. '*A serial killer is on the loose in Kings Richington!*' *What are our police doing about it?*' *How many more innocent people must die before they catch this dangerous madman?*'

* * *

Two mornings later at nine o'clock, Professor Davenport was already drinking coffee with the team when Inspector Dawes arrived. Bugsy did the introductions.

'Professor, this is Inspector Dawes. He's heading this investigation.'

She got up from where she had been perched on the edge of PC Jackson's desk and held out her hand. She was nearly as tall as Jack. and, in modern parlance, very "fit." 'Good morning, Inspector Dawes. I'm Cressida Davenport, Head of Psychology and Criminology at Richington University. Pleased to meet you.'

'Good morning,' Jack heard himself squeak in a voice he didn't recognize. He couldn't have been more surprised if she'd said she was Boudicca, Queen of the Iceni. She was stunning. Thick blonde hair twisted into a topknot, smart business suit and very high heels. Her make-up was impeccably applied, attractive but not over the top. Jack felt a twerp for assuming Professor Davenport would be a man. Corrie would certainly take a dim view of his chauvinism. He recovered quickly. 'I'm so glad you could come, Professor. I'm sure you must be extremely busy, but we could really use your help.'

'I've already asked your team to call me Cressida. I hope you will too, Inspector. Your sergeant and Simon have already filled me in on the progress you have made already. And I realize the press is making a ghastly meal of the situation, as only they can.'

'I'm afraid the editor of the *Richington Echo* always has it in for us. He probably had a parking fine or a speeding ticket ten years ago and hasn't got over it. We're either not doing enough or we're too heavy-handed.'

She laughed. 'Damned if you do and damned if you don't. Well, shall we make a start?'

'The sooner the better.'

She walked to the front and the team gathered round, notebooks and laptops at the ready.

'Criminal profiling was first used in the UK in 1986, but it's been around in one form or another for much longer. Back in the Middle Ages, inquisitors tried to profile heretics. But the first offender profile was put together in the 1880s by detectives of the Metropolitan Police on the personality of Jack the Ripper.'

'Never caught him, though, did they Professor?' challenged Mitch.

Quick as a flash, she countered, 'No, but then I wasn't on that case.' There was appreciative laughter. 'What I'm seeking to do is define the behaviour of your serial killer before he reaches the height of his criminal career.'

'Does that mean you think he's going to carry on killing?' asked Aled.

'Most certainly. He'll carry on until we stop him. That means we need to predict his next move before he makes it. We shall use the evidence in hand from the four murders already committed to anticipate what he may attempt to do next.' She sipped some water. 'As part of evaluating the evidence, I propose to try to reconstruct the events of the crimes. My familiarity with thought patterns and correlated behaviours will hopefully fill in the gaps in the story told by the evidence, particularly if it's mainly circumstantial.'

She looked towards Jack. 'We might also try to communicate with him via the media. This has risks but it has proved quite successful in the past. These criminals are basically attention-seekers and welcome being given a name by the press and becoming famous or, should I say, infamous.'

* * *

Once the media got wind of the timings of the murders, the perpetrator was predictably dubbed 'The Moon Killer.' Hardly original, but the press loves an epithet.

'Smoke and mirrors,' muttered Garwood, when Jack had explained what was happening. 'Do you know how much she charges, this Professor Davenport? A bloody fortune, that's how much.'

'I doubt if it's much more than she earns for lecturing at the university, sir.'

'So what do we get for our money?'

'Well, the physical product is a report of her findings. This includes an assessment of the killer's motives, his behaviour patterns and a theory as to why he commits the crimes in the first place.'

'Yes, but will it help us catch him, Dawes? That's what I want to know.'

* * *

'What's she like, this Professor Davenport?' Corrie was serving up another of her experimental recipes for supper. Jack had no idea what it was. It looked like spam fritters floating in pond weed, but it obviously wasn't.

'Intelligent, committed to her subject and determined to get results. I like her.' He took a mouthful of food and quickly washed it down with a gulp of stringent Pinot Grigio.

'No, I mean what does she look like?' Corrie was well aware that Jack was an attractive man in a rugged sort of way. He had a big nose and jug ears and an off-centre grin — his features having been somewhat rearranged during his early rugby-playing years — but his charm was undeniable. He was Corrie's second husband, the first having left her for a Scandinavian fitness instructor with her own sauna and muscles like Superwoman. It would be fair to say that it hadn't been a heartbreaking parting, but this wasn't the case with Jack. To lose him would be devastating. She looked at him sideways. 'Has she got a nice figure?'

Dangerous territory this, thought Jack. 'What are we eating, sweetheart? It's delicious.'

'Pan-fried sweetbreads in a crumb, with pea purée, *sous vide* shallots and asparagus spears. Is she attractive?'

'Yes, in a superficial sort of way. The lads at the station think so, anyway. What's a sweetbread before it becomes supper?'

'A lot of people mistakenly believe they're lamb's testicles. In fact, they're two separate glands — the thymus gland from the throat and the pancreas gland from the stomach. Shall we invite her to dinner, and her husband, if she has one?'

'Yes, if you like, darling. Is there any cheese?'

* * *

Over the next week, they studied the blown-up photograph of the Richington Under-21 football team from twenty years ago. There was no guarantee that these were the only men that the Moon Killer intended to murder, but it was a start and it was all they had by way of a heads up. Professor Davenport was delighted.

'Now this is really useful. You say four of these men have been murdered already and with a tampon in the throat? You see, that tells me a lot. As I mentioned before, serial killers need to experience some form of release from a kill. Disabling their victims then watching them choke slowly gives them the maximum satisfaction.'

'Yeah, but why a tampon?' asked Bugsy.

'Oh, probably just random to start with. Easy to get hold of and conceal. Impossible to trace back, you can buy them anywhere. Could have been any device, but it worked, so he carried on using them. The applicator would make it easier to shove it right down his victim's throat.' She studied the photo closely. 'Have you been able to identify all these men?'

'No, unfortunately not,' said Jack. 'We had a vague idea that if the Richington United management had any back records, they might be able to tell us, but there was a fire about fifteen years ago that destroyed everything. Nobody at the new stadium remembers any of the Under-21s from twenty years ago.'

'Ah, now this is where we use the press,' said Cressida with enthusiasm. 'Some of them are bound to read the *Echo* and if not them, their relatives. We'll get them to publish this photo and ask the public to contact the police if they know anyone in it. Tell them it's for their own safety to come forward. A bit like when you've bought a washing machine and you find out they've been catching fire. What do you think?'

'Won't that scare the shit — er, daylights out of them?' suggested Bugsy. 'They might see it as a kind of hit list.'

Cressida shook her head. 'I think we should do it. We won't publish any names or details of the team. Then, when we know who they are and where they live, we can warn them. Of course, some of them might have moved away, like your Joe Roberts, but they may have relatives still living in the area.'

CHAPTER ELEVEN

The editor of the *Echo* handled it in his usual lurid way. '*Are you one of these men? If so, you may be in danger. The police have been unable to trace them. Can you help?*' The article didn't name the men or the team, so as to minimize timewasters. There was a telephone number to call with information. The result was a deluge of phone calls, mostly of dubious significance, but each had to be followed up.

'What's the tally, Taffy?' Bugsy looked at the list on the board.

'So far, we've got one "possible," which we're following up. Other than that, a sad call from a mother who says the centre midfield was her son who died in a motorbike accident five years ago, and a woman who says she was engaged to the left-back but he emigrated to Australia the day before the wedding, so now he's in the outback.'

Bugsy grinned. 'Many timewasters?'

Aled pulled a face. 'Aren't there always? One old guy reckons his dad served with the goalkeeper at Dunkirk, even though I told him the photo was dated 1999, and a lovely old dear swore the young man on the end of the back row was Elvis Presley. I'm surprised we haven't had more genuine identifications, Sarge. You put a group photo on Facebook, for example, and ask, "Where are they now?" and they all come crawling out of the woodwork.'

'Look at it this way, young Taffy. The photo is twenty years old, and the faces are blurred. We didn't release any names. These blokes' features could have changed significantly over the years — certainly, the dead ones' had. And even if a bloke recognizes himself, there are any number of reasons why he might not want to come forward. Ex-wife trying to trace him for money, on the run from debt collectors, bodies buried under the patio, who knows? My personal view is that if I saw a photo in the paper of my old football team and the headline says they may be in danger, and then I saw on telly about four murders by a serial killer, I'd put two and two together and I wouldn't be in too much of a hurry to put my name in the frame, would you?'

* * *

One of the 'possibles' was a vicar with a parish on the outskirts of Richington, a deprived area where he had hoped to make a difference. Five years on, the only difference he had made was that attendance had dwindled to almost nothing, there was the constant threat of closure and one of the local thugs had put a brick through the stained-glass window. He had responded to the police request to come into the station for a chat.

DC Fox put the Reverend Hugh Toplady in the interview room with a cup of tea and a plate of custard creams. Mitch and Bugsy went in to interview him, while Gemma took notes.

'Thanks for coming in, Vicar. Nothing to worry about, but we just need to confirm that you were one of the lads in this photograph.' Bugsy handed it over.

'Oh yes, that's the one that was in the *Echo*.' He pointed to the right-back. 'That's me.' He looked a little wistful. 'You may not think it now, but I was very fit, back in the day.'

'What do you remember about the team back then?'

'We had a good life. Some of the lads were a little, shall we say, exuberant, especially on a night out. I had an invalid mother to look after, but it was good to let off steam with my teammates from time to time. For a while, I had hopes of finding a job as a professional, but I found God instead.'

'Are you married, sir?' asked Bugsy.

'No, Sergeant. Sadly, the right lady never came along when I was young, and now I don't seem to have the right job for attracting women.' He gave a wry smile. 'The sum total of my family is an elderly aunt in Hove. I go to see her occasionally, when I can manage a day off.'

Mitch hesitated, unsure of how to proceed without alarming this quiet man. It was hard to believe that someone might want to kill him. 'Has anything unusual happened lately, any threats or situations that have made you worried or uncomfortable?'

'No more than usual, Constable. In my parish, there's always some kind of violence or bloodshed, on an almost daily basis. I take it you're referring to the other articles in the *Echo* about the Moon Killer.'

'That's correct, sir,' said Bugsy. 'Four of the men in this photograph have been murdered.'

'And you think I might be next? Don't worry, Sergeant, I don't need police protection. My God will protect me.'

'Let's hope he's right,' said Bugsy after he'd gone. 'Only another week or so to the sixteenth of July and the next full moon.'

* * *

At Corrie's insistence, Jack invited Professor Davenport and her husband, Oliver, to dinner the following weekend. To her surprise, Corrie found she liked Cressida very much. As Jack had said, she was a sensible, intelligent woman with a strong work ethic but also an irreverent sense of humour and a vivacious personality. Oliver, her husband, was pleasant enough but clearly lived in her shadow. He obviously adored her. The two couples found they had much in common, having married late in life due to career commitments, and neither had children.

The wine flowed freely and the food was excellent.

'You're an amazing chef, Corrie. I'm so impressed. I can knock up a dinner party with a lot of help from M&S, but I couldn't produce a meal like the one you've just given us.'

'Hear, hear,' said Oliver, spooning up the last of his pudding. 'Lovely dessert. What is it?'

'It's a champagne and raspberry posset with Chantilly cream. It's one of Jack's favourites. It's a popular choice at Coriander's Cuisine, too.'

'That's your catering business, isn't it? I googled you. I'm hoping I can book you for our next dinner party. We have to entertain Olly's banking chums from time to time.'

'It would be a pleasure. Just give me a ring.'

'And you have an online fast food outlet too?'

'That's right. Corrie's Kitchen. Useful when you both get home late and don't want to cook.'

Oliver helped himself to more Stilton. 'It's an interesting name, Coriander, and very appropriate, too. But Corrie Dawes — corridors? That must be a bit awkward.'

'Not really, Oliver, I'm used to it by now.'

'No more awkward than Cressida. My students at the university call me Sid.'

'What made you choose to study psychology?' asked Corrie.

'Probably the same thing that made you take up cooking. I liked it and I found I was good at it, good enough to make a living out of it anyway. Also, when I was a teenager, I had a few issues with depression — didn't we all? — and I thought it would help me to get over it if I understood what had caused it.'

'I can't imagine you being depressed,' said Corrie. 'You're so lively and vibrant.'

'Oh, that was years ago. I'm fine now, thanks to my work — and Oliver, of course. We try to do lots of fitness

74

classes together in our spare time. Martial arts, weights, kettlebells and training for marathons. That helps with your mental state too. And profiling is very important to me. I believe very strongly in justice and it's my contribution to helping catch criminals who need to be punished. I know that isn't a very fashionable view but it's mine, and I make no apologies for it.'

'And nor should you,' said Jack. 'I'm with you one hundred per cent. With your help, I hope to put a stop to the madman who's trying to bump off a football team from twenty years ago.'

'Is this the one the press is calling the Moon Killer?' said Oliver. 'The man's evil, irredeemable. He should be locked up for the rest of his life, but I guess the do-gooders will find him unfit to plead and he'll spend the rest of his life in a nice, comfy hospital for the criminally insane with visits from someone like my wife, trying to find out what makes him tick.'

'Enough shoptalk,' said Jack. 'Who'd like a cognac or liqueur?'

* * *

'What a pleasant couple,' observed Corrie, after they'd seen them off in a taxi. Throughout the evening, she'd had a vague feeling that she'd seen Cressida somewhere before, but thought that she couldn't have, unless she had simply passed her in the street. 'We have a lot in common, don't you think, Jack?'

'Yes, I suppose we have.' Jack had drunk rather too much wine and was struggling to get his right arm in the left sleeve of his pyjamas.

'She's very glamorous,' said Corrie, remembering the designer blouse and Christian Louboutin shoes.

'Is she?' asked Jack. 'I didn't really notice.' He wasn't so drunk that he didn't know an elephant trap when he saw one.

'Oliver's in banking,' said Corrie. 'He offered to help if the business ever needed a loan. Wasn't that kind?'

'Bankers aren't kind, Corrie, they're money-savvy and he could spot a good prospect. It's the umbrella theory — banks only offer you an umbrella when it isn't raining, or something like that. Have you done something to my pyjama jacket?'

CHAPTER TWELVE

16 July. The Buck Moon

The Church of St Stephen needed some serious renovation, both inside and out. The Reverend Hugh Toplady sat in his tiny office in the old, rundown house that served as a vicarage and pored over the parish accounts. They weren't looking good. As the Church of England was keen to turn around falling attendance figures, he had tried to enlist the help of lay volunteers, charged with taking the word to the streets — a form of modern-day missionary work. He rapidly discovered that the people of Lower Richington didn't volunteer for anything unless there was money at the end of it. Ideally, he saw himself spending more time in contact with people, spreading the word of God and tending to his parishioners' spiritual needs. But the only spiritual needs they seemed to have were the ones that came out of a bottle in the Goat and Garter.

Sometimes he wished he'd married. Bishops preferred their vicars to be married, and a wife could be such an asset in a failing ministry. He'd been engaged a few times before he was ordained but it hadn't worked out, mainly due to his promiscuity. He'd told the police sergeant that when he was young, the right lady never came along. In truth, too many of them had come along. He liked to think of himself as the farmer in the 'Parable of the Sower.' He'd scattered his seed far and wide, wherever and whenever he could. Rocky places, hot places, thorny places, he hadn't been fussy. In truth, not so much a sower of seed as a total letch, he believed was the modern terminology. None of it had borne fruit as far as he was aware, so here he was, like John Keats's 'knight-at-arms' — 'alone and palely loitering'.

He sighed and put the books away in his desk drawer. It was late, half past midnight, and he was tired. But it had always been his habit to start and end the day with personal prayers in the church. He slipped a coat over his cassock and crossed the road. The night was lit by a full moon that streamed through the stained-glass window, where the brick had made a sizeable hole, so he didn't bother to light candles. It all cost money.

He knelt before the altar and began to give the Lord thanks for his calling, his health and his deliverance — which was rather premature, as it turned out. He heard a noise behind him. Sometimes one of the many homeless people in Lower Richington would try to sneak into the church to spend the night, but mostly in winter. This was a warm night in July. The vicar rose to his feet and turned around. There was someone there. He couldn't see who it was, even in the moonlight, so he called out.

'Hello. Can I help you?'

They were to be the last words he would utter in this world, words offering help.

* * *

It was around ten o'clock in the morning when the church-warden, a plump grey-haired lady, arrived at the vicarage to remind Reverend Toplady that the parish's end of year accounts were well overdue. The deadline for submission was 31 May and the bishop was concerned. Privately, she thought the vicar wasn't really up to the job. He was decent enough, she supposed, but she couldn't help thinking there was 'something of the night' about him. If the bishop had asked her to be more specific, she couldn't have provided anything concrete. It was just an uneasy feeling she had.

When there was no reply to her knocks on the vicarage door, she decided he must have gone across to the church. She knew it was his habit to pray last thing at night and first thing in the morning. Ten o'clock was a little late, though, as he had a Bible reading class at ten thirty.

She found the church unlocked, so he was obviously inside. You didn't leave a church unlocked overnight in a parish such as this. Thieves would have taken everything that wasn't nailed down, including some things that were. She could remember, during the previous vicar's ministry, coming in to find they'd taken the carpet from the entire length of the aisle and the curtains from around the altar. She supposed they had ended up on a stall down the market. Although what a thief could do with fifty hymn books, she couldn't imagine.

She pushed open the heavy church door and called out, 'Are you here, Vicar? You're going to be late for Bible reading and the bishop wants the parish accounts.'

She smelt him before she saw him. It was an abattoir smell, sickly and sweet.

Reverend Toplady lay on his back on the steps of the chancel, the front of his cassock soaked through with blood. His arms were outstretched, as if nailed to a cross. She ran screaming all the way back to the vicarage, where she rang the police.

* * *

By the time DI Dawes and DS Malone arrived, it was a crime scene, carefully preserved until the SOCOs and Dr Hardacre arrived. The police constable, ashen and queasy, lifted the tape for them to approach. They put covers over their shoes and pulled on disposable gloves. It was a harrowing scene, but the worst part for Jack was the expression on the corpse's face — utter terror and disbelief.

The scene had even shocked Bugsy. He spoke softly. 'Blimey, Jack, whatever happened to the poor bugger?'

'If you gentlemen would stand back, I could probably hazard a guess.' Dr Hardacre had arrived, closely followed by her bag carrier, Marigold Catwater. Suitably garbed, she knelt beside the vicar and gently lifted his cassock. The sight underneath caused every man in the church to swallow hard and clench his buttocks. Dr Hardacre didn't flinch, however. She turned to Miss Catwater, who looked like she might throw up. 'Marigold, will you see if you can find the victim's penis and testicles, please? I don't imagine the killer took them away with him. You might follow that trail of blood leading to the font.'

The vicar's genitals were, indeed, in the font. Dr Hardacre placed them carefully in a sterile container. The telltale blood and saliva around the vicar's mouth prompted her to produce forceps and after some probing, she took out the inevitable tampon with a flourish, like a rabbit pulled from a hat.

'Are you anticipating many more of these murders, Inspector? Only the mortuary is filling up rather. If you and your team could catch who's doing it, we could maybe release a few bodies for their funerals.'

The SOCO team went about their business, combing every corner of the church for evidence, anything that might help catch the killer.

Jack was sure they wouldn't find anything. Experience showed that serial killers could become careless, overconfident, certain they'd never be caught. But not this one. *He's too smart to make mistakes*, thought Jack. They would have to match his cunning and sheer nerve if they were to trap him.

* * *

Dr Hardacre's post-mortem report made gruesome reading. Reverend Toplady had sustained a vicious blow to his genitals, possibly a punch, which would have caused severe pain, and the shock would have caused him to lose consciousness. His penis and testicles had been sliced off with one flourish, using something very sharp — possibly a butcher's knife — which had not been found. It had not been possible to establish which had come first, death from bleeding out or choking on the tampon.

'There was certainly a lot of blood,' said Bugsy. They were back in the incident room and DC Williams was adding the latest murder to the whiteboard.

'I can't believe it,' said Aled, appalled. 'He was only in here a couple of weeks ago, drinking tea and eating custard creams in the interview room. Now he's lying in the mortuary, with his wedding tackle in a jar.'

'None of the others had their genitals chopped off,' observed Simon. 'I wonder why the killer did it to the vicar. Why was he different?'

'Good question, young Jung-Freud. When we catch the bastard, you can ask him.'

'He's also the first one that we were able to speak to while he was still alive,' observed Mitch. 'The first knowledge we had of the others was after they were dead.'

'That makes me feel like we let him down,' said Gemma.

'Who had the last known sighting?' asked Jack.

Aled consulted his notes. 'The members of the Mothers and Toddlers group. They meet in the church hall every Monday afternoon for two hours of tepid cups of tea and screeching babies.'

'CCTV?'

'There were cameras installed, sir, but according to the churchwarden, Reverend Toplady kept them switched off. He believed that places set aside for private devotions, such as churches, fell within an especially sensitive category and worshippers would not expect to be filmed while praying.'

'Someone will have to go to Hove and tell his elderly aunt,' said Jack. 'Maybe the church will see to it. Unless anyone has any other ideas, I don't see much mileage in interviewing the poor old soul. She'll be upset enough as it is, and I doubt there's anything she can tell us that would help catch the killer.'

* * *

Jack had called a team meeting. Five deaths. Only six more members of the Richington United Under-21s to go and the Moon Killer would have wiped out the whole team. Professor Davenport usually came to work on a bike, but this morning she decided to run. She arrived in professional looking sports gear and disappeared to the ladies. She re-emerged looking immaculate.

'Sorry to be late. I'm training for a marathon and I daren't let up. Please carry on, folks.'

'In your last book, Professor Davenport, you say that anyone can commit murder,' said PC Jackson. 'Does that mean anyone can become a serial killer?'

'Absolutely, Simon. No one is immune to acts of insanity, including you and me. I believe that every person has a certain threshold. If that is overstepped, things can happen that no one would ever have imagined. I call this the "dark side of the soul," or the "grim face of a human being."'

'Are we talking about evil here?' asked Jack.

'Well, Jack, evil feeds off it. This shadow is the unloved, the negative side of one's personality, with all the socially unacceptable characteristics that go with it.'

'Do socially unacceptable characteristics include leaving a mouldy sausage roll in the evidence cupboard?' asked Gemma.

Bugsy grinned. 'Is that where I left it? I wondered where it had gone.' He looked at his watch. 'It's half an hour since I had anything to eat. I can feel my blood sugar rushing down into my boots.' He pulled a fruit pie from his pocket, unboxed it and took a bite.

'What's our next step, Professor?' asked Jack, glad of a few moments of light relief to temper the sickening shock they were all feeling.

'Inspector, I've been studying the modus operandi and the victims. My view is that we need to look wider than the men in the photograph. Of course, they fit a pattern, but that's not the only one. I fear that if we focus only on them, the killer will strike elsewhere and catch us on the back foot.'

Jack felt like he'd been on the back foot since March. He was starting to wonder if he'd ever get on the front foot. But he supposed she did have a point. This professor was an expert, a well-respected speaker and author.

'What do you suggest? The next full moon is on August fifteenth.'

'Then we have less than three weeks to outsmart him. I've built up a picture of this man, much like the Metropolitan Police did with Jack the Ripper. There is no clear-cut definition or model of a serial killer. However, this gives us a reasonable description that I hope will help us piece together his motivation and, eventually, catch him.'

CHAPTER THIRTEEN

The final profile report was detailed and thought-provoking. Professor Davenport presented it to the team, with Chief Superintendent Garwood present. As he said, 'He wanted to see what he was getting for his money.'

'Our man is young — I'd say late twenties to early thirties — and clearly very strong. I would guess at least six feet tall and well-built. He almost certainly works out. He always disables his victims with just his hands or feet, no weapons. It's very likely he was abused as a child and may experience sexual gratification from the domination and humiliation of his victims.'

'No semen was found, Professor,' commented Simon.

'That doesn't mean he didn't produce any, Simon, he just kept it to himself. He is a unique brand of individual who will make special efforts to elude detection.'

'He's certainly done that very well,' said Garwood peevishly.

'He has the appropriate biological predisposition, modified by his psychological make-up, that was present at a critical time in his social development.'

'What the hell does that mean?' muttered Garwood.

She had excellent hearing. 'It means, Mr Garwood, that he has been gradually working up to murder for most of his life.'

'What do you think triggered it after the full moon on the twentieth of March, Professor?' asked Jack.

'Could be any of a number of traumatic life events. Maybe his mother died, his wife left him, his football team was relegated . . . who knows? But it was enough to tip him over the edge. And you don't yet have any evidence that Wayne Jenkins was his first murder, do you? In my experience, by the time the police realize they have a serial killer on their hands he's done a couple of others already.'

'Might the football team element be relevant?' DC Williams felt sure it must be. He didn't believe in coincidences.

'Possibly.'

'So he somehow got hold of a photograph of the Richington United Under-21s from two decades ago and decided to eliminate them all?' Garwood was unconvinced.

She eyeballed him. 'How do you know he wasn't one of the team? He could be in that photo himself. We haven't identified them all yet.'

'In that case, he'd be a bit older than your estimate, Prof. He'd have needed to be at least sixteen to be in the team.' Bugsy had checked with the current coach. 'That would make him at least thirty-six.'

'As I said, Sergeant Malone, profiling isn't an exact science. We work mostly on the balance of probabilities — a bit like when you play the football pools online.'

'If he could kill with a punch or a kick in the right place, why didn't he do that instead of choking them to death with a tampon?' Jack was hard pressed to think of anything nastier.

'The tampon, Jack, is a metaphor for both life and death. By using it as a murder weapon, our killer is demonstrating a profound "loss of self," a fundamental form of suffering in the mentally ill. He is struggling with a tragic event in his life. A tampon is essentially feminine, so as I previously suggested, it could be the loss of his mother, wife or daughter. Or maybe, he has gender issues and in trying to suppress his feminine side, the murders represent his efforts to express the inexpressible.'

She summed up her findings. 'I'd say we're looking for a powerful man, unhappy childhood, poor education, no moral compass. Probably works in a labour-intensive industry such as car manufacture, construction, the fitness industry, even agriculture. He is a true sociopath who lives by his own set of rules and morals. Dangerous? Yes, I'd say so. Treatable? I doubt it. Evil? Certainly. But you wouldn't be able to pick him out in a crowd.'

After she'd gone, Jack asked, 'What did you make of that, Bugsy?'

'Bollocks,' came the reply.

* * *

Jack's car was in for a service, so Bugsy gave him a lift home. He could have borrowed one from the pool but didn't, in case it might be needed for something more urgent.

'Bugsy, how nice to see you,' said Corrie. 'Are you staying for supper? There's plenty.'

'No, thanks, Mrs D. I'm meeting my lady friend tonight. We're going to the pictures to see *Downton Abbey*. Iris liked the series on the telly, so we thought we'd . . .' He tailed off when he realized that Jack and Corrie were staring at him, open-mouthed. He stared back. 'What? . . . What? Have I got snot on my nose or something?'

Corrie steered him into the kitchen and sat him on a chair. 'Why didn't we know that you have a lady friend, Bugsy?'

'Maybe,' hazarded Jack, 'because it's actually none of our business.'

Corrie ignored him. 'Tell us all about her. How did you meet her?'

'On a dating site. Not one of those daft ones for youngsters, you understand. It was for middle-aged professionals, like me. My neighbour's son showed me how to do it. You have to upload a photo and your details, then list your hobbies and—'

'Yes, we know how it works,' said Corrie impatiently. 'Tell us about your lady.'

'Her name's Iris and she works as a receptionist down at the health centre. She's a widow, couple of years younger than me, with a grown-up son.' He pulled out his wallet and showed them a picture.

Blimey, thought Jack. *He's even carrying a photo of her. It must be serious.*

'You must bring Iris to supper, so we can meet her. How about next Saturday?' Corrie intended to give this lady friend a good going-over. She had become very fond of Bugsy over the years and she didn't want to see him messed about.

'Thanks, Mrs D. She'd like that. Must be off. Don't want to be late.'

'Well,' said Jack, after he'd gone. 'What d'you make of that?'

'I'll tell you after we've met her.'

'Sweetheart, why shouldn't Bugsy have a girlfriend?' asked Jack, reasonably. 'He's a grown man with active loins.'

Corrie frowned. 'I think we should leave his loins out of it. I'm more concerned about his pocket. I hope she isn't after his money.'

'Bugsy hasn't got any money. He spends it all on food. Why do women always think other women are after a bloke's money?'

'Because some of them are, and we can spot them better than you.' She took a casserole from the oven and the room was suddenly filled with mouth-watering aromas. 'I just want him to be happy, that's all.'

'So do I, darling.' Jack picked up his knife and fork. 'Can I eat some of that or is it more horse jollop?'

* * *

It was turning out to be one of the hottest Julys on record. Everyone in the station was in shirt sleeves except Detective Chief Superintendent Garwood. He sat in his sumptuous, oak-panelled office, wondering what had happened to the engineers. He had summoned them half an hour ago to come and fix the air conditioning. He needed to control the intolerable heat and humidity before it ruined the patina on his gleaming mahogany desk. He took out a snowy white handkerchief and gave it a quick buff up.

This serial killer was causing him considerable angst. He was sure he was getting an ulcer. Cynthia said he was a hypochondriac. She also accused him of having obsessive compulsive disorder, which was nonsense. He repositioned his blotter to dead centre and lined up his pens, exactly parallel. Then he took a deep, steadying breath. Now that Sir Barnaby's threat to replace him had been temporarily averted, he could at least sleep properly again but his bowels had not yet returned to normal. Whisky helped. He opened his drawer, took out a bottle of Glenfiddich single malt and poured himself a healthy dram.

This Professor Davenport might be trendy in terms of modern policing, but he failed to see how she was helping to identify and arrest the killer. Four murders in as many months and as far as he could see, they were no further forward. It might work on those terrible police dramas on the television that Cynthia loved so much, but this was real life policing. His money was still on Dawes cracking the case, although he wouldn't tell him as much. There was something about the man, his superior attitude and subtle modesty, that made Garwood feel inferior and at a disadvantage. He'd considered having the blasted man transferred but he couldn't afford to do that, because most of the successful clear-up results of the MIT were down to Dawes, and Commander Sir Barnaby knew it.

There was a knock and the door flew open as if someone had given it a kick. Malone burst in, files under his arm, and carrying a bacon roll balanced on top of an overflowing mug of tea. He dumped the roll on the bit of desk Garwood had just polished and took a swig of his tea, sloshing some on the very expensive carpet.

'Inspector Dawes is just coming, sir. Got held up on the phone.'

Garwood slid his whisky glass into his in-tray and covered it with the files Malone had brought. He looked at him with distaste. The man was a disgrace. Shirt sleeves, baggy, unpressed trousers and a scruffy football scarf. Who wore a scarf during the hottest July temperatures on record? 'What are you doing here, Malone?'

'You wanted a progress report, sir? Ten o'clock sharp, you said.'

There was a tap on the door and Inspector Dawes came in. 'Sorry I'm late, sir. I've been on the phone to the assistant manager of Richington United. I'm still of the view that the answer lies there somewhere. Despite what Professor Davenport says, it's too much of a coincidence that all the victims were members of that football team twenty years ago. She may be right that there are other deaths that we don't know about, but I think we have to work with what we've got. There's another full moon in two and a half weeks. I don't want to be standing over another poor devil with a tampon stuck in his throat.'

'You're right, Dawes. Get over there and have a poke around. But try not to upset anyone. I still have an executive box there.'

Seconds after they'd left, Malone put his head back round the door. 'Careful with those files in your in-tray, sir. You don't want to spill your whisky.' He grinned and hurried out.

* * *

The assistant manager, Mr Harris, took Dawes and Malone into his office and organized coffee and biscuits.

'I'm not sure I can help you, Inspector, but I'll certainly try. The *Echo* has made a big thing of the Richington United connection to the serial killings since they published that team photo. They've even posted it on their Facebook site. It reflects badly on the club, even if it was twenty years ago. There has been so much in the media recently about historic abuse in football only now coming to light after many years, and the public always thinks the worst. And we rely on supporters and benefactors to a great extent, to keep going. We've already lost Mr Bryce-Jones and it doesn't look like his widow is going to continue with the donations.'

The coffee and biscuits arrived. *Chocolate digestives*, observed Bugsy. *They can't be doing that badly.*

'That photo in the *Echo*, Mr Harris. You didn't recognize anyone on it?' wondered Dawes.

'No, I'm afraid not, Inspector. I've only been here eighteen months.'

'Nothing in your archives that might be useful?' tried Malone.

'Sorry. All destroyed in the fire fifteen years ago.'

The canteen tea lady came in with her trolley, to see if they wanted a top-up.

'No, we're fine thank you, Eileen.'

'I wouldn't mind one of those iced buns, since you're here, love,' said Bugsy.

She came around the desk with a bun on a plate and as she put it down, she glanced at the photo, which was much bigger than the one in the *Echo*.

'You've been here a long time, Eileen,' said Harris. 'Do you recognize anyone?'

She plucked her spectacles from their customary location on top of her head, put them on and picked up the photo. She studied it for some moments. 'No, sorry, dear. They'd all have been before my time.' She paused, then pointed. 'Hang on. I know him, though. That one right at the back.' She laughed. 'He's got a bit of a paunch on him now but he's still very fit.'

'Do you know where he went?' asked Dawes.

'He didn't go anywhere, dear. He's still here.'

CHAPTER FOURTEEN

Vic Walker was the Assistant Coach. They found him out on the pitch, coercing a dozen or so young men to dribble balls in and out of posts set up for the purpose.

'Come on, you lazy buggers. You look like a lot of girls. Let me see some speed! Keep your eyes on the ball!' He was taking backhanders from the parents of most of these lads, in return for getting them a place in the first team. If they didn't improve, his nice little earner could be threatened.

Mr Harris went outside with them. 'Walker,' called Harris, 'these police officers would like a word. Hand over training to the captain and come inside, please.'

'Why? What am I supposed to have done?'

'Nothing, as far as we're aware, Mr Walker,' said Dawes.

'We think you might be able to help us,' added Malone.

Dawes observed that he was a big man, still powerfully built, but in places, the muscle had turned to flab. Once inside, they showed Walker the photograph.

'Is this you, Mr Walker?'

'Yeah, that's me,' he said grudgingly. 'I played right wing. I could run, back then. Long time ago now.'

'The name on the back is Victor Bailey.' Dawes showed him.

'Yeah, well, that's because my dad buggered off and my mum married again. Walker's my stepdad's name.'

'Didn't you see this photograph in the *Echo*, Mr Walker? We asked anyone who recognized themselves to come forward. There were contact details.'

'No, I don't read the *Echo*. The sports pages are lousy.'

'When you were playing football for the Richington Under-21s, do you remember anything unusual happening to any members of the team? Anything at all?'

'No, it's years ago. I have a job remembering what happened last week, mate.'

'So you can see no reason why five of these men have been murdered?'

He looked shifty, his eyes darting from Dawes to Malone. After the initial glance, he studiously ignored the photo. 'No, I can't. We never did nothing dodgy.'

Dawes thought that was a strange response. He hadn't implied that they had collectively 'done something dodgy,' so why should Walker assume that's what he meant?

'Were you even *aware* that five members of your old team, presumably your friends back then, had been killed?'

'Yeah, I saw something about it on the telly, didn't I?'

'And that didn't worry you?' said Dawes, surprised. 'It would worry me.'

'Why should it? Whatever they'd been up to, I wasn't part of it. I wouldn't know nothing about it. It was a long time ago.'

'Yes, so you keep saying,' said Malone. 'Are you still in touch with any of them?'

'Course not. People moved on, got proper jobs.'

'Except for you,' suggested Dawes. 'You're still employed here.'

'Yeah, and if I don't get back to work, I won't have a bloody job much longer, will I? Can I go now?'

They thanked the Assistant Manager for his cooperation and left him with contact numbers in case anything else came to light that he thought might be useful.

Once the two police officers had let him go, Walker hurried back into the stadium to the locker room. He emptied all his belongings out of the locker, stuffed them in his bag and legged it. He'd read everything he could about the murders, knew all the details from the news on the telly and social media. Far from not being worried, he was seriously scared. He had a pretty good idea why those blokes had been killed. He thought he even understood the choking thing with the tampon. What he didn't know, what he couldn't even guess, was who might be doing it. But one thing was certain, he wasn't going to hang around to find out.

As Bugsy and Jack reached the car park, they saw Walker hurry to his car, throw his armload of sports gear in the boot and roar away.

'I wonder where he's going in such a hurry,' said Bugsy. 'Shall we follow him?'

'No. He hasn't done anything, as far as we know. But my copper's nose says he didn't tell us the whole truth. And despite what he said, that is one very frightened man.'

* * *

Professor Davenport had been given police security clearance so she could come and go as she pleased. She decided to call into the station on her morning run to see if there had been any progress since her last visit. The incident room was quiet. Everyone was out interviewing potential witnesses or taking statements. Only PC Jackson and a couple of others were in, manning the phones and trawling the police database for anything relevant.

'Hi, Simon.' She sat beside him. 'Sorry if I stink a bit. I've just run ten miles.' She drank from her water bottle. 'Have we identified any of the others in that photo yet?'

'That's what I'm doing now. T.I.E.'

'And in English, we say . . . ?'

Simon grinned. 'Trace, Interview, Eliminate.' Although he'd been told that the recent discovery of Vic Walker still working at Richington United had to be kept quiet, that surely didn't mean he couldn't tell Cressida. She was, after all, the expert they had brought in to help with the case. 'But we have found someone of interest. It was more by accident than design. Inspector Dawes and Sergeant Malone went to United's stadium to see if anyone there had remembered anything and they found a bloke who'd been in that 1999 team. He's still working there as a coach.'

'Really? That's excellent. What background do we have for this guy?'

Simon pointed to the whiteboard where everything they knew about Vic Walker, including a current image, was displayed. She read all the details, making notes on her phone.

'I see his father left his mother when he was only sixteen. Then she remarried. What does that tell you, Simon?'

'Er . . . he suffered a traumatic life event at a critical time in his social development. He might see his mother marrying again as losing her. She could be the feminine element that you mentioned in your report — and that could translate into a "loss of self."' Simon had read the report several times. He thought the professor was brilliant.

'Very good. Vic Walker could be our killer rather than another potential victim. We need to tell Inspector Dawes. I have a strong feeling about this, Simon. I think we have our man!'

* * *

Vic Walker didn't intend to hang around waiting for the full moon so that some nutter could pick him off like the other poor sods. After the visit from the cops, he went straight from Richington United football ground to a cheap boarding house in the red-light district of Lower Richington. There was a girl there that he visited regularly. Jenny would let him stay until he could find somewhere more permanent. He'd go back for his stuff later, once he felt it was safe.

CHAPTER FIFTEEN

Corrie had pulled out some of her best dinner party recipes for Saturday night. She wanted to impress Bugsy's lady friend, but she also wanted to show Bugsy how much she and Jack valued him as a friend.

'Blimey, matching plates,' observed Jack, laying the table. 'You're really pushing the boat out. What are we eating?'

'Scallop and tuna ceviche, to start.' She was polishing the cutlery with gusto.

Jack had no idea what ceviche was but knew better than to ask. No doubt he'd find out later.

'Then fillet of beef foie gras, parsley purée and Madeira sauce. I know how much Bugsy likes beef.'

'That's true.' Jack thought parsley purée sounded like more pondweed but didn't say so.

'I managed to get some courgette flowers. Wasn't that lucky? We're having those stuffed with ricotta, sultanas and pine nuts.'

'Lovely, darling, we're going to eat flowers.' Jack remembered eating a daffodil for a bet during his carefree student days, but this was something new.

'For pudding, I've made a chocolate tart — Bugsy loves chocolate — with salted caramel and pistachios.'

'Is that the one with green bits on top?'

'That's right.'

'One of my favourites.' At last, something Jack recognized.

'We're having a selection of canapés when they arrive, so make sure you have the wine chilled.'

'Yes, darling.' Now that was something he could cope with.

Corrie stopped suddenly and smacked her forehead. 'Oh my God, Jack. I've just had a ghastly thought. What if Iris is a vegetarian? Or even worse, a vegan?'

'That doesn't make her a bad person, sweetheart.'

'I know it doesn't. It just means she won't be able to eat anything. I should have checked with Bugsy.' She shot off to the kitchen to see if she could rustle up a vegan meal from Corrie's Kitchen if the worst came to the worst. But she didn't need to. It turned out Iris had the same tastes in food as Bugsy, just not in the same quantities.

Bugsy declared himself starving when they arrived and scoffed three canapés in quick succession before Jack had even uncorked the champagne.

Iris scolded him, laughing. 'I'm pretty sure you're not meant to put them in whole. Ooh lovely! Champagne!' she enthused. She was a sociable lady. While not attractive in an obvious way, she made up for it with a cheerful disposition. Corrie took to her immediately, much to Jack's relief. Iris was clearly fond of Bugsy. She called him Mike, so that must be the name he'd put on the dating site.

Corrie was impressed to see that he was wearing a clean shirt, a jacket with no food down the front and had foregone the scruffy Arsenal scarf.

'What a lovely home you have, Mrs Dawes,' Iris said.

'Please, call me Corrie.'

The ceviche went down really well, although neither Jack nor Bugsy had a clue what they were eating. However, Iris did. 'I can taste coriander in your lime juice marinade.' She smiled. 'Coriander is such a lovely name, and so unusual.'

'I have a twin brother called Basil,' explained Corrie. 'Our mother was stuffing lamb noisettes when she went into labour, so she called us after the herbs she was using. I'm just grateful she wasn't stuffing a chicken or we'd have been called sage and onion.'

Everyone chuckled and the evening was shaping up to be very jolly. By the time they'd finished pudding, everyone was replete except for Bugsy, who was tucking into his second slice of chocolate tart.

'Bugsy — I mean Mike — tells us you have a son, Iris.' Corrie found mothers always liked to chat about their children, and Iris was no exception.

'His name's Dan, he's thirty-six and he's a doctor. He has a lovely wife, Cheryl, and I have two wonderful grandchildren — James and Olivia, five and seven. I'm very lucky.' She paused then, a little embarrassed, knowing that Jack and Corrie were childless. She wondered if it was a painful subject, but it never had been.

'They're great kids,' agreed Bugsy.

'You've met them, Bugsy?' asked Corrie. 'How lovely.'

'They adore Mike. He's wonderful with them.'

Well, who would have thought it? mused Jack. *Bugsy had hidden depths. Maybe all those years he'd devoted to the police service, he'd really have liked a wife and family.*

'Have you always lived in Kings Richington?' asked Corrie.

'Oh yes. It's my home. It's where Dan grew up and where my late husband had his practice. He was a doctor, too. We did think at one point that Dan might have wanted to become a footballer. He was very talented as a youngster. But we were glad when he gave it up to study medicine.'

Jack was doing the sums in his head. Twenty years ago, Dan would have been sixteen. They lived in Kings Richington and he showed signs of being a talented footballer. Jack really didn't want to go there. Especially not at a dinner party.

After Bugsy and Iris had gone, around midnight, Jack and Corrie were having a nightcap.

'I think that went very well, don't you?' said Corrie. 'Iris seems perfect for Bugsy. She's introducing him to all the things that have been missing in his life — hygiene, dry-cleaning, a good deodorant.' She glanced at Jack, suspecting he wasn't listening. He was totally lost in thought. She tested him. 'Of course, what he really needs is a twenty stone drag queen with hairy legs and halitosis, don't you agree?'

'Mmm, yes, darling, I'm sure you're right.'

'I know what you're thinking.' Corrie could always pick up on Jack's mood. 'That Iris's son might have been in the "doom team," back in 1999. Surely Bugsy would have considered that and checked it out?'

'Not necessarily. It's not something you'd throw into the conversation in a new relationship. "Oh, and by the way, darling, was your son in the Richington United Under-21s in 1999? Only if he was, there's a chance he might be on a serial killer's hit list."' He finished his drink. 'Oh, ignore me, sweetheart. Just because the lad showed signs of being good at football doesn't mean he had anything to do with the sinister Richington United lot. He was probably just captain of the school first eleven. These serial killings have got me spooked and now I'm seeing potential victims around every corner. Let's turn in.'

* * *

At the same time, out in the country at Davenport Hall, Oliver Davenport sat shuffling papers at the big oak desk in his study. As a merchant banker, it was his job to help industry grow and survive. He was finding it difficult to keep pace with the emerging problems facing the corporate business world. The rapidly changing financial environment was challenging at the best of times, but lately he'd been distracted by his concern for Cressida. He was ten years her senior and acutely aware of the fact. He'd kept himself physically fit — they both had. They worked out together, regularly, and their marathon training was punishing. Cressida drove herself relentlessly and he feared she would burn herself out if she didn't let up. Tonight, she was out at her kickboxing class and intended to run a few miles before coming home.

They had married two years ago on a beach in Malibu. No relatives or friends invited, just the two of them, and it had been magical — for him, anyway. He knew he was a stuffy sort of bloke with a stuffy job, and by the time he'd met Cressida, he was well set in his ways. She was vibrant, beautiful and had a brain the size of a planet. When they met, she had just been appointed Head of Psychology at the university at the age of thirty. When she finally agreed to marry him, three years later, it had transformed his life. He still couldn't believe that a woman like her would want to be with a man like him. He would have given her the world, but he couldn't give her the one thing she wanted most. Nobody could. He poured himself another brandy, knowing he'd already had more than enough.

CHAPTER SIXTEEN

It was less than a week until the next full moon. DI Dawes called a team meeting, including Professor Davenport but not the Chief Superintendent. Meetings that included Garwood always seemed to run into the sand due to differing opinions on budget priorities or any proposed activity, however justified, that he feared might reflect adversely on his next promotion.

DI Dawes stood in front of the whiteboard which was, by now, crammed with pictures, names and arrows linking information. They had a state-of-the-art Smartboard in a cupboard somewhere. It had been one of Chief Superintendent Garwood's brainwaves. He had included its acquisition as evidence of his cutting-edge use of IT at his last annual review with Sir Barnaby. His theory was that it was ideal for teams to use. Anyone could jump in and add notes, he said, move pictures around and perform mouse functions with just a finger. Four people could use it at the same time. A Smartboard was the sign of a smart team! What had actually happened was that Bugsy knocked it off its trolley and stood on it, erasing a whole week's work with his boot. It never worked properly after that, so they went back to the whiteboard and pens.

'What do we think about this man?' Jack pointed to the picture of Vic Walker.

'I reckon he's going to be next,' said Aled. 'We should give him police protection on Thursday, when it's a full moon.'

'I disagree.' Professor Davenport stood up. 'I believe there is every chance he is our serial killer, Jack. He fits the profile perfectly. Ask yourself, why didn't he come forward in response to all the media hype?'

'That's right, sir,' agreed Simon. 'Walker admitted, eventually, that he'd seen the team photo and he knew that five of the men on it had been murdered. I don't know about anybody else, but if that had been me, I'd have shot into the nearest nick before you could say the words "Moon Killer."'

'Unless you *were* the killer,' insisted Cressida.

Simon nodded enthusiastically. She was amazing, so intuitive and skilled.

'Assuming you're right, Professor, what's his motive?' asked Jack.

'PC Jackson and I have discussed this, haven't we, Simon? There are critical life events in Walker's past that point to escalating psychosis. Something relatively trivial like a full moon could trigger an uncontrollable urge to kill.'

'Does he have any family, sir?' asked Aled.

Jack looked to Bugsy. 'Sergeant Malone?'

'Not that we could find, guv. He lives alone in a one bedroom flat over a Chinese takeaway in Kings Richington High Street. Should we get a double-u and turn it over?'

Jack thought about it. 'We don't really have enough evidence for a warrant, apart from the compelling profile from Professor Davenport, and magistrates tend not to be convinced by anything other than hard evidence. Sorry, Cressida. Tell you what we could do — we could make a courtesy call on Thursday on the pretext of duty of care. We'd merely be taking appropriate and proportionate action to protect a member of the public from potential harm. At the same time, we could have a good snoop around.'

It might have worked, but when Jack and Bugsy arrived at Walker's flat on 15 August, he wasn't there. The door was open and they could see he'd cleared out and taken all his stuff with him.

Bugsy summed it up. 'Either he's the killer, like the Prof said, and he thinks we're getting a bit too close — my gut says he isn't, incidentally — or he's shit-scared he's going to wake up dead with a chalk mark around him.' Bugsy sniffed — chicken chow mein, special rice, king prawn curry. 'Since we're here, Jack, shall we get a Chinese?'

Jack rolled his eyes. 'You're a bottomless pit. And we've a job to get on with.'

'We could ask what they know about the bloke who lived in the upstairs flat and if they have a forwarding address.'

'Oh, go on then.'

The Chinese gentleman on the counter in the takeaway was a bit short on English conversation. He was OK with Bugsy pointing to numbers on the menu, but when it came to questions about the tenant of the upstairs flat, he was baffled. He went out to the kitchen and came back with a young woman.

She smiled amicably. 'Hello, can I help? My father says you want to know about Vic.' Her English was perfect, with a rather attractive Cantonese inflection.

'That's right, love,' said Bugsy. He didn't flash his warrant card. Sometimes there were people working in such establishments who'd rather not advertise the fact, especially to the police. 'We've got some property belonging to him that we'd like to return. We've been upstairs but he's moved out and taken all his stuff with him. I don't suppose you have a forwarding address?'

'No, I'm so sorry. He came down to tell us that he was moving away about a fortnight ago. He took a couple of suitcases and a few bits and pieces. I asked if he wanted his post sent on, but he said he wasn't sure where he'd be staying.'

'How did he seem, in himself?' asked Dawes.

'I thought he was very nervous. Anxious to get away. I don't think he'd have come in at all, except he wanted some food to take with him.'

'OK, thanks, love.' Bugsy picked up the bag containing their food and the girl gave him a complimentary bag of rice crackers.

They were almost out the door when she said, 'Someone else has been asking after him recently.'

They turned around and came back in. 'Do you know who it was?' asked Dawes.

'No. Only that it was a man in running gear. You know, jogging trousers and a hoodie. He wanted to know the same as you — did I have a forwarding address for Vic.'

'Can you describe his face?' asked Malone.

'No, I'm sorry. It was more or less covered by the hood. And anyway,' she said with a smile, 'I'm afraid you all look the same to me.'

CHAPTER SEVENTEEN

15 August. The Sturgeon Moon

It was midnight. Vic Walker was sitting in Jenny's bedroom watching football on TV and eating beans out of a tin. She was out with a punter and it was an all-nighter, so he was alone. He'd been there over a fortnight and had only just calmed down. It was reassuring being in a whorehouse, in a weird kind of way. He could hear punters coming and going on the landing. At least there was always someone about, even in the middle of the night.

He'd taken sick leave from his job with Richington United, planning to stay off just until the cops had caught the lunatic who seemed intent on killing them all. Five of them were dead already. Surely they would catch the maniac soon. If he knew who it was, he'd tell them, but he hadn't a clue. He hoped it wouldn't take too long. Without the hefty bribes from the club, his income had drastically reduced.

There was a gentle knock on the door. It sounded like one of Jenny's regulars who didn't know she was already on a job.

He shouted, 'She's not here, mate.'

There was another knock, louder this time. Obviously, the bloke wasn't going to take no for an answer. Walker put down his baked beans and went to open the door.

'Look, mate, Jenny isn't—' His face twisted in horror. The figure was all in black with a leather mask covering his face. All Walker could see were the eyes, cold and deadly, like a snake. Panicking, he turned to get away — the last mistake he'd ever make. He felt a massive blow to the nape of his neck. It rendered him helpless, but not unconscious. He began to plead, 'Please, it wasn't my fault. We were just kids. We didn't know what we were doing. You've got to believe me. Please . . .'

He guessed what was coming next. His attacker was ramming something down his throat with black, gloved hands. He was choking, gasping for breath, but it was hopeless. He felt consciousness slipping away, oblivion descending and then, nothing.

* * *

When Jenny returned at seven o'clock the next morning, she was tired, hungry and in need of a shower. She unlocked the door and called out, 'Morning, Vic. I'm back.' She hung up her coat behind the door. 'God, he was a boring old git. Kept telling me about the important cases he'd tried when he was a judge, down the Bailey. And he didn't half snore. I don't suppose you've cooked any breakfast? I'm starving—'

Walker lay cold and stiff on the rug in front of the fireplace. His face was contorted, eyes bulging, and there was blood and saliva around his cyanosed lips. Jenny ran back out onto the landing, screaming, white with shock and close to fainting. Doors opened and heads popped out to see what was happening. Her neighbour from the room next door put a coat around her.

'Jenny, whatever's the matter?'

Jenny couldn't speak, just pointed.

The neighbour, an older woman, went inside. There was little point in testing for a pulse. The man was obviously dead and it didn't look like natural causes. In her line of business, you did get the odd death, on the job, so to speak, but that was normally a stroke or heart attack due to unaccustomed excitement. Much safer if they just had sex with their wives. Awkward, certainly, but not criminal. This man had clearly met a violent death. She went back out onto the landing, closing the door behind her, careful not to leave prints on the latch. Reluctantly, she asked, 'Jenny, you didn't kill him, did you?'

Jenny shook her head vehemently.

'Then we have to call the police. You mustn't touch anything. Come into my room and we'll wait for them there.'

By now, men were making hurried exits all down the landing, some still pulling on their trousers. This was not where they wanted to be found when the police arrived.

* * *

When the call came through to the MIT, the day after the Sturgeon Moon, they were almost expecting it. Jack had had a bad feeling about Walker ever since they'd visited his empty flat the previous day. Why had he cleared out over a fortnight ago without telling anybody where he was going? And, more to the point, who was the man in the takeaway, asking for his address?

'For Christ's sake, how many more?' pleaded Bugsy. 'This man's not a serial killer, he's an exterminator.'

'That's six now,' said PC Jackson, pragmatically. 'One more than Jack the Ripper's canonical five. I say canonical because I don't believe we know for certain exactly how many women the Ripper killed, just as we can't be sure how many men this man has killed. We only know about the ones that have been found.'

'That's right, young Jung-Freud,' said Bugsy. 'Cheer us up, why don't you.'

* * *

By the time DI Dawes and DS Malone arrived at the crime scene, Dr Hardacre was already there with the team of SOCOs.

'This is a bit off your usual patch, Inspector, a boarding house for ladies of the night.' She got to her feet assisted by Miss Catwater, who was fascinated. Not with the corpse but to be in a sex worker's bedroom. One of the forensic team was going through the contents of the wardrobe. There were all kinds of uniforms from schoolgirls to nurses — whips, chains, handcuffs and ball gags. Marigold recognized this last item from a magazine she'd bought, purely for research, of course. She was always keen to broaden her knowledge of pathology and she would have claimed, if challenged, that this included potentially dangerous sex toys.

Jack looked up and down the corridor outside. 'I don't suppose there's any CCTV?'

'Do me a favour, guv,' said Bugsy. 'In a bawdy-house? What do you think?'

'What happened to him, Doctor?' asked Jack, wearily.

'It's our old friend, blunt force trauma, in this case to the back of the head, at the base of the cerebellum. It would have caused mortal damage but not necessarily killed him straight away. I'd put the time of death between eleven o'clock last night and two this morning.'

'Weapon?' asked Malone, hopefully.

'No, Sergeant. In my opinion, this blow was administered by a powerful fist wearing a sturdy glove, possibly leather reinforced with metal. I'll examine for traces at the post-mortem, but I doubt if I'll find anything significant, and we'd need to find the glove in order to match it. The victim was finished off by our killer's *coup de grace*.' She held up a tampon in bloody forceps. She gestured to the team busily turning everything over and putting things in evidence bags. 'I fear these poor souls are wasting their time. This room must be teeming with detritus and DNA from half the male population of Kings Richington.'

'That's a good point, Doctor,' Jack said. 'DNA is the surest way we have to prove someone committed a crime. Our killer has been careful to choose places where there's likely to be a host of DNA from strangers. Jenkins was killed in the park, Bryce-Jones in a lavatory, Aduba in his gym, Roberts in a fish shop and the Rev Toplady in a church. Isolating his DNA would be like finding a needle in a haystack.'

'Smart,' said Malone. 'This bastard's smart.'

* * *

Jenny had been the last person to see Vic Walker alive and the first person on the scene after he was dead. Although there was no reason to suspect she was the killer, Jack needed to interview her in order to maintain correct Code of Practice. He didn't want to bring her into the station unnecessarily, so they went to see her in the room next door. Her neighbour had made her the customary shock remedy, hot sweet tea, but she was still trembling violently. DC Fox had joined them, as Jack felt a female officer might be less intimidating.

Gemma started gently. In her view, Jenny's choice to be a sex worker was just as valid as her own choice to be a police officer. Each occupation came with risks.

'Jenny, can you tell us what happened in your room last night?'

She swallowed hard. 'No, I can't. I wasn't there.'

'How did you know the deceased?' asked Dawes

'Vic was one of my regulars.'

'But you weren't there with him last night. Why was that?' Gemma asked.

'No. I had an all-night appointment booked with someone else. I went out at ten o'clock and got home at seven this morning. That's when I found him.'

'If he wasn't booked in with you,' asked Malone, 'why was he in your room?'

'He rang me about a fortnight ago, asked if he could come and stay for a bit. I got the impression he was on the run from someone. He said the police weren't after him, so I thought it would be OK. He paid me well, even though he was off sick from work. I just assumed he wanted to avoid someone he owed money to. I never thought they'd actually kill him.' She sniffed a bit then, thinking that if she'd been there, they might have killed her too.

'I have to ask you this, Jenny,' said Gemma, 'we need the name and address of the man you spent the night with. It's just to keep our records straight.'

'Are you saying I need an alibi? You don't think I killed Vic, do you?' She was horrified at the very idea.

'No, not at all. It's just police procedure to tie up any loose ends.'

'Well, he told me he was a High Court judge down the Bailey, but I don't think he can be. He's really old and kept falling asleep. I call him Binky and he calls me Lola. He takes me to his club in Chelsea. I've no idea where he lives, I've never asked. It doesn't do to be too inquisitive in my job.'

They left it there as there didn't seem to be any point in questioning her further. There was no doubt in any of their minds that this was the work of the Moon Killer. Gemma told her that she wouldn't be allowed back in her room for a few days and if she requested it, the police would find her alternative accommodation.

* * *

On the way back to the station, a puzzled Jack went through what they knew.

'Walker was killed in a sex worker's bedroom, not in his own flat. It was empty when we went there yesterday. He'd taken all his belongings and Jenny told us he was intending to hide out from someone for a while. She thought it was a debt collector — we know it was our tampon killer. Despite the stonewalling when we interviewed him, Walker knew the killer was after him. He might not have known who it was, but he was pretty certain he was a target.'

'Right, guv. What are you thinking?'

'How did the killer know where he'd gone? The young lady in the Chinese takeaway didn't tell him.'

'Good point. Maybe he left a forwarding address with another neighbour,' offered Bugsy.

'That would be a bit risky. I think he was scared and just wanted to disappear for a while until the dust settled. But who might he be obliged to tell?'

'His employer,' said Gemma. 'Richington United would have to know. He'd have to notify them if he wanted to keep his job and get sick pay.'

When they got back, Jack phoned the Human Resources manager at the football club. He told her Walker had been found dead that morning and she was suitably shocked.

'He'd been on sick leave for a couple of weeks, but I had no idea it was that serious. The poor man.'

Jack asked if she had known about his change of address.

'Yes, Inspector. Walker did notify us of his change of address. It's one of the requirements to apply for sick pay.'

'Did anyone else know where he was?'

'Well, the police did,' she said, confused. 'An officer phoned and asked for his address. Said it was necessary to ask him some more questions.'

'And you told him?'

'Yes, of course. Why wouldn't we cooperate with the police?'

'Did you get the name of the officer who called you?' Jack knew what the answer would be before she said anything.

'No, I'm afraid not. I didn't think to ask.'

'When was this?'

'Some time yesterday afternoon, I think.'

'Might you be able to trace the number of the caller from your records?'

'I'll try, but wouldn't it be easier for you to do that from your end? Trace any calls made to us from your station?'

'Probably, but since you're on the line, would you mind?'

She was gone a good five minutes. 'I'm sorry, Inspector, this is very strange, but the caller must have used a pay-as-you-go.

You know, one of those phones where you don't have to give your name and address when you buy it or when you activate the SIM. There's no account holder — it's anonymous. The number simply didn't register. It's how our system works. Why would one of your officers ring us from an unregistered phone?'

Why indeed, wondered Jack.

CHAPTER EIGHTEEN

'So much for my carefully worked-out hypothesis,' said Professor Davenport on Monday morning. 'I'd have staked my reputation on the killer being Walker. Everything about his profile pointed to it. His behaviour, his personality traits, life experiences and deep-rooted mental issues all led me to conclude that he was our man. But I was wrong. Sorry, guys.'

'Your profile might have said it was him, Prof, but my gut said it wasn't,' declared Malone.

Dawes agreed. During his years in the police service, he'd acquired a wealth of knowledge about criminal behaviour and human nature. It might not match the professor's psychological profiling technique, but it had served him well. The Moon Killer was cunning, astute and calculating, indicating a mind far sharper than Walker's. The fact that he'd killed six times and still managed to evade detection and arrest meant he had carefully planned his movements long before he made them. Jack would have been surprised to learn a man like Walker was capable of planning what he was having for his tea. And there was that vital ingredient — evil. There was definitely a very dark side to this killer. They were looking for a man who took calculated risks to achieve his aim, to kill all the men in the football team. The only thing Jack couldn't fathom was why.

PC Jackson leapt to the professor's defence. 'You mustn't blame yourself, Cressida. The profiling was accurate and inspired. It was a conclusion that any professional might have come to. And as we know, it isn't an exact science. We worked on the balance of probabilities.'

'It's back to the drawing board, folks,' announced Bugsy. 'Or in this case, the whiteboard. We have to work on the probability that this bastard intends to strike again in September. Do we know when the full moon will be?'

Aled had downloaded the whole moon calendar on his computer back in May when three murders had been committed and the smart money said there would be more. 'The moon will reach its full phase at 5:32 on Saturday morning September fourteenth. It's a Harvest Moon, apparently.'

'Blimey, that's early,' Bugsy said. 'Still, I don't expect the killer will be setting his alarm to make sure he slaughters his next victim exactly on time. We just need to be on the alert from Friday night to Saturday morning.'

'One last thing,' said Jack. 'Did anyone telephone Richington United to ask for Walker's change of address?'

There was a puzzled chorus of, 'No, sir.'

* * *

Corrie Dawes was working in the busy kitchen of Coriander's Cuisine. The scorching summer temperatures continued unabated and with all the ovens going, it was very hot. She took a water bottle outside for a breather.

Corrie had built up a thriving catering company since she first started a few years ago. Back then, she had one small unit on the Kings Richington industrial estate. She'd been a one-woman band, but a dynamic one, sometimes working twelve-hour days to get her business up and running. Jack's work schedule was somewhat similar, so the time they spent together was limited. But she comforted herself with the thought that they always ate well. Over the last two years, she had expanded to include Corrie's Kitchen and now occupied three large units on the same estate.

She had cleverly identified a niche market for customers who didn't want posh dinner party menus but something within their price range that had a better production quality than other fast food outlets. Corrie's Kitchen fulfilled all the requirements of the demographic that it was intended to target. It also meant that she came into contact with a varied cross-section of Kings Richington's citizens.

'The vans are loaded up, Mrs D. Shall I let them go or do you want to check them first?' Carlene was Corrie's deputy and an excellent chef.

'No, that's OK, Carlene. Let them go, I know they'll be fine.'

* * *

When Corrie interviewed her for the job, Carlene had presented a vastly different image to the smart young lady she had become. She'd had several studs in her face and ears, tormented magenta hair and a relentlessly bare midriff, regardless of the season. When Corrie had asked her why she wanted the job, the answer had been succinct but honest.

'I want to work in caterin' but I never got enough GCSEs to deliver pizza, so it was either this or chopping giblets down the abattoir.'

These days, the tormented magenta hair was just a memory and all the hardware had gone. She wore whites and her shiny chestnut bob was tucked under her cap.

For Corrie, having a deputy she could trust and leave in charge when necessary meant she had more time to help Jack with his murder investigations, although he insisted that he could manage perfectly well on his own. Corrie acknowledged that he was a first-class detective, but she reckoned he lacked the devious treachery that she could contribute to catching criminals.

She had to admit that she seemed to be a magnet for danger. In the course of 'assisting' him, she had been poisoned by a psychotic botanist, bashed unconscious with a ballroom dancing trophy, held hostage on the parapet of an eighty-foot tower and had her shoulder dislocated by the avenging Sword of Islam. None of it had dampened her irrepressible enthusiasm for getting involved. But this latest case was scary. She wondered, with a slight shudder, if she had unknowingly sold food to the Moon Killer. Do serial killers buy food from catering companies? Did Jack the Ripper nip down to the Ten Bells for a plate of mutton and potatoes?

'That's them gone, Mrs D.' Carlene returned. 'And the next batch of pasta meals is nearly ready.'

'Carlene, what do you think of this serial killer who's on the loose in Kings Richington?'

'It's time the police caught him, that's what I think. Six people he's killed, and he's still out there. It's like Jack the Ripper, reborn into the twenty-first century. Mind you, they never caught him, neither. But then back in 1888, they never had things like DNA and computer matching like we do now. What with the full moon malarkey and the things he stuffs down their throats, he's a right creepy sod.'

'You seem to know a lot of the details, Carlene.'

'It's all over social media, Mrs D. I bet the bloke's loving it, being called the Moon Killer and outwitting the police.'

'Yes, but surely you don't kill people just to get attention? He must have another agenda.'

'According to Facebook, they'd all been footballers once. I reckon that explains it.'

'Does it?'

'Yeah. Lots of people wouldn't mind getting rid of football. Just look what it does to your telly. You sit down at half past seven to watch 'Corrie,' and instead of the music and that picture of all them chimneys, there's some rubbish about 'EUFA Champions League,' and some old blokes are sat round a table talking about a game of football like it's important. So I miss my soap just because of a stupid football match. And another thing, why do footballers think it's macho to spit? It's not — it's disgusting. And as for that thing they do when they close one nostril and blow snot out of the other — yuck!'

You can rely on Carlene to tell it like it is, thought Corrie, amused. 'So you reckon the Moon Killer just hates footballers?'

'Yeah, and the full moon sends him loopy, so he has to kill another one. Bugger only knows what the fanny-fillers are all about.' She opened the door to go back inside to her batch of spaghetti bolognese. 'Still, there's one good thing about it, Mrs D.'

'What's that?'

'He hasn't killed any women yet.'

CHAPTER NINETEEN

Oliver Davenport was in the kitchen making supper when Cressida got home from Richington University. She had been working long hours preparing for the new intake of freshers due at the end of the month. He didn't know if she was still profiling for the police. She hadn't mentioned it for a while. Oliver was able to work from home two or three days a week, so on those days, he liked to cook for her.

She looked tired and pale when she came into the kitchen. Still wearing her jacket and outdoor shoes, she sat down on the nearest chair. He stopped chopping carrots and poured her a glass of wine, sensing something was wrong. She normally gave him a kiss when she got home.

'Oliver, I have something to tell you. Promise me you won't be upset.'

Now he was really worried. 'What is it, my darling? Tell me.' He sat beside her and held her hand.

'I'm going into hospital tomorrow. I have to have surgery.'

'Oh, Cressida, my darling. Has it come to that? I'm so sorry. Will you have to lose everything?'

'Yep.' She took a deep swallow of her wine. 'The whole lot — uterus, cervix, ovaries and fallopian tubes. My complete set of reproductive tripes. So that makes it final, doesn't it, Olly? The end of the road. No chance of your becoming a father now. Not with me, anyway.'

'Darling, that doesn't matter to me. Your health is far more important. We've known for a while that there was little chance of you being able to carry a child to term, even if you did get pregnant. This just draws a line under it, so we can move on and get you strong again.'

'It means we can't run the marathon as soon as we planned.'

'Yes, and all our classes must stop, until you're completely recovered. You've been really punishing your body lately, my darling — kickboxing, Muay Thai, Aikido, and the weight training will definitely be out of bounds.'

'Oliver, please don't keep telling me what I can't do. You make me sound like a total fitness freak. We've tried to counterbalance our mainly sedentary lifestyles with plenty of exercise, that's all. And I'll get back to it as soon as I can. It doesn't mean that you have to stop, though.' She stood up and refilled her glass. 'I'm going to have a bath.'

'All right, my darling. Dinner in half an hour.'

She left Oliver deep in thought. Cressida, the love of his life, was hurting right now. He didn't know how to help her, whether he even could. She was a professor of psychology, so she knew only too well how such life events could impact on someone's state of mind. All he could do was support her, and he vowed to do that with whatever action was necessary.

* * *

The news that Professor Davenport was in hospital having a hysterectomy travelled fast. PC Jackson got the information from some old chums at the university. He told Inspector Dawes and Jack told Corrie.

'Poor Cressida, that's awful, and she's still so young.'

Jack nodded. 'Yes, she's about thirty-five I believe. No chance of a family now.' He was looking at the full moon charts that DC Williams had printed out for him and planning how to deploy his team on 14 September.

Corrie put down the saucepan she was holding with rather more clatter than was necessary. He wondered what he'd said.

'Jack, women aren't just baby machines, you know. It is possible for us to be fulfilled in life without a litter of sprogs clinging to our skirts. Cressida is a career woman and a very successful one. I don't imagine the loss of her womb will hold her back in the slightest. I shall visit her in hospital and take her some fruit salad from the Cuisine.'

Jack wondered if he'd been crass. Had Corrie been secretly wanting children herself for the past years? 'Corrie, do you wish you'd had a child?'

She laughed. 'Good Lord, no. I already have one. I've got my hands full looking after you.'

* * *

Cressida's room in the private hospital was filled with flowers and cards telling her to get well soon. She'd come through the operation extremely well, according to her consultant. She was young and extremely fit and would be able to go home in a few days. Oliver sat by her bedside, his heart aching for her. She was absolutely determined that she'd be back to normal as soon as possible, and he was worried she'd overdo it.

'What did the consultant say about convalescing?'

Cressida reached for his hand. 'He said I should take it easy for six weeks or so. No kettlebells, kickboxing, that kind of thing. I'm sure it won't take me that long to be fit again. But you don't have to stop. I don't want you to vegetate on my account.'

Oliver had no intention of carrying on without her. 'No, my darling. It wouldn't be the same without you.'

Corrie tapped on the door. 'Is it all right to come in?'

'Yes, of course,' said Cressida. 'How kind of you to come, Corrie.'

Oliver pulled another chair up to the bed. 'Lovely to see you again.' He kissed her on the cheek which she thought was a little odd, since they'd only met once at the dinner party, back in July. She didn't have him down as a demonstrative kind of man.

'I've just brought you a bit of fruit. You obviously have plenty of flowers.' Corrie handed her a pretty dish containing some superb exotic fruit salad.

'Corrie, thank you so much.' Cressida was genuinely pleased. 'Your mouth gets so dry in hospital. That's perfect.'

They chatted, mostly about work. 'How is Jack progressing with catching the serial killer?' asked Oliver. 'I haven't seen much on the news lately.'

'That's because there isn't much to broadcast. Obviously, the investigation is ongoing and other avenues of enquiry are being explored. Goodness, listen to me. I sound like a police spokesperson. That's what happens when you've been married to a copper for years.'

'Please tell Inspector Dawes I'm sorry I've had to bail out, but I'm happy to have another crack at profiling as soon as I'm allowed back to work,' said Cressida.

'And that won't be for some weeks,' insisted Oliver. 'Darling, weren't you going to ask Corrie to cater the dinner party we had arranged on the thirteenth of October? You won't be fit enough to manage it.'

'Yes, could you, Corrie?' asked Cressida. 'It's for a few of Oliver's banking cronies and their wives. We could always cancel it, but I'd rather not.'

'Of course.' Corrie was pleased to help. 'Just tell me what you want on your menu and I'll bring it round on the day, in good time for you to transfer it to your own dishes and pretend you made it yourself.'

'I was rather hoping you and Jack would join us,' said Oliver. 'I know my lot can be very boring for Cressida. At least she'll have someone interesting to talk to.'

Corrie looked shocked. 'You mean you're going to ask me to eat my own food? That's a terrible thing to do to a chef.'

Corrie left, having agreed to email some popular menus to the Davenports so they could decide. She still had an uncanny feeling she'd seen Cressida before, in a totally different setting. She tried hard to recall it, but her mind wouldn't oblige.

CHAPTER TWENTY

September 14. The Harvest Moon

It was the night of the full moon. All leave had been cancelled and the MIT had been told to expect to spend all night in the station.

'This time we'll be ready for him, guv,' said Bugsy, more in hope than expectation.

'Well, we're getting closer,' said Mitch.

'Are we?' asked Aled. 'How do you make that out?'

'Well, the first four of his victims were dead before we even got to them. At least we managed to interview the last two when they were still alive.'

'Yeah, but he still got 'em, didn't he?' said Bugsy. 'It'd be nice if we could get to the next one before he does.'

'I wish we knew who the others were on that photograph,' said Dawes. 'At least it would give us a fighting chance. There are no more names on the back that we haven't already identified, and some of the ones that are left are fuzzy and very young looking.'

'Professor Davenport said it might not necessarily be one of them.' Simon thought they'd have a much better chance of catching the killer if they followed Cressida's thinking. 'We don't know whether he's responsible for any of the other unsolved murders on our books.'

'You could be right, son,' said Bugsy. 'But I reckon Big Ron would have noticed if they'd had a tampon stuck in their throats. Dr Hardacre may not be the pinnacle of pulchritude, but she's bloody good at her job.'

Sergeant Parsloe fixed a map to the whiteboard. It had red stickers all over it. 'There you are, Inspector. That's a schedule of the extra area cars that uniform have deployed tonight. They've been told to look out for anything unusual and to be vigilant. No sitting in the car eating fish and chips until it's time to knock off. There are new shifts waiting to take over.'

'Thanks, Norman. We'll have a full team here waiting to respond as soon as anything kicks off.'

The only thing that kicked off that night was the Arsenal versus Spurs match that some of the lads were watching on their phones. The Harvest Moon peaked at 12:33 a.m. and as it came and went, everyone held their breath. It was unlikely the killer would strike right on time, but you never knew.

For the next hour, some of the uniform men played cards, Aled was messaging his girlfriend and Simon was reading up on Criminal Law and Procedure in readiness for his next fast track posting. Mitch and Gemma were playing chess on a travel board.

Jack had ordered food from Corrie's Kitchen at his own expense to keep everybody fed. Corrie drove it to the station in the van, with Carlene helping to unload. Corrie wouldn't normally have asked any of her staff to deliver food in the middle of the night, but Carlene was keen to help. She looked around at the somnolent incident room.

'Nobody's carked it yet, then?'

'No, but there's still time, Carlene.' Jack never ceased to be amused by her graphic turn of phrase. 'We won't know for sure until the morning.'

'See you at breakfast, then, Jack.' Corrie collected the containers from Jack's desk, then collected Carlene from the desk of a handsome young constable. It was three in the morning by the time they got back home. Carlene had a self-contained bedsit above one of the Cuisine kitchens. She was especially proud of it and kept it spotless. It was the first real home she'd had after a long, sad history of care homes, bail hostels and halfway houses.

As she got out of the van, she asked, 'Inspector Jack — he will be all right, won't he?'

'Yes, of course he will, Carlene. Don't worry. Get some sleep and don't come in until lunchtime tomorrow.'

But Corrie had been thinking exactly the same. If it came to a confrontation with the killer, who she knew was seriously powerful, never mind evil, Jack would wade straight in without hesitation. Bugsy would be close on his heels; Kings Richington's answer to Batman and Robin. She hoped they would stay safe.

* * *

A week later, with no reports of any bodies having been found, murdered or otherwise, Jack had to concede that the Moon Killer had missed his target for the first time since the whole sickening business began on 20 March some six months ago. It was either that or he had disposed of the body and it would come to light at a later date. But he didn't think that was the case. It wasn't how this killer worked. He needed his crimes out there, not hidden away. It had been Professor Davenport's theory that the killer wanted to scare the other men in the photograph into iden-tifying themselves and their whereabouts to the police and the media.

As if reading his thoughts, Bugsy said, 'You know, guv, we've been assuming all along that the killer knows all the men in that football photo and where to find them. What if he doesn't? What if he knows some of them, the ones he's killed, but he's waiting for the others to get the wind up and come forward?'

'Exactly what I was thinking, Bugsy. Even though we would guarantee them anonymity, we can only go so far. And even if we put any potential victim in a safe house, these things have a habit of leaking, either through relatives or someone wanting to sell the information to the tabloids.'

'It could be that he's run out of victims and he's waiting until we find them for him. I'm still struggling with his motive, Jack. I know he's a nutter — you'd have to be to do what he does. But even nutters have some sort of reason, a pattern of some kind.' Bugsy called across to PC Jackson. 'Oi, Jung-Freud. You're studying for your next fast track — what are the three elements of a crime that we need for a conviction?'

'Means, motive and opportunity, Sarge.'

'Well we've established means — the bloke is strong enough to put 'em down with his bare hands. As for opportunity, he makes his own. He studies their behaviour, then picks the right time. But what the buggery is his motive?'

'In criminal law,' quoted Simon, 'motive in itself isn't a required element to prove any crime. However, the legal system typically allows motive to be proven to make the accused's reasons for committing the crime more plausible, especially when motive is obscure.'

'Yes, all right, son. Nobody loves a smartarse. All the same, I think if we could find out his motive, we'd be a long way towards catching the bastard.'

* * *

The last days of September were uneventful after the build-up of expectations mid-month. It was as though the team had been holding its breath and could now let it out. Chief Superintendent Garwood had endured a couple of very uncomfortable meetings with Commander Sir Barnaby, who demanded to know why this lunatic wasn't in custody yet. They had six bodies in the mortuary that couldn't be released for burial while the case was ongoing. Relatives were writing to their MPs. What was the Murder Investigation Team doing? The overtime budget had gone through the Home Office roof and what had he got to show for it? He implied that if Garwood didn't tell them to get off their arses and do some real work, he might have to replace the whole lot of them, including Garwood.

CHAPTER TWENTY-ONE

13 October. The Hunter's Moon

When the next full moon rose on 13 October, Jack wasn't taking any chances. Just because the killer hadn't struck in September didn't mean they could assume it was all over. Jack the Ripper may have stopped in the autumn of 1888, for whatever reason, but the public still demanded protection.

Teams of officers from the MIT and uniform were deployed, as last time, despite the chief superintendent's complaints about the overtime budget being hugely overspent. Jack claimed it was good for public relations, as Garwood could claim that no expense had been spared in the police's determination to protect the good folk of Kings Richington. That had sounded rather good, so Garwood decided to use it in his next report to Sir Barnaby.

The full phase of the Hunter's Moon was at 5:08 in the early evening. If the MIT wasn't exactly holding its collective breath once again, there was certainly a tense atmosphere. At midnight, it was still quiet. Area cars had phoned in with reports of noisy domestic rows, drunks being chucked out of pubs and various other petty crimes but no dead bodies, and no sign of anyone behaving suspiciously with a packet of tampons.

Jack ambled across to Bugsy, who was working his way through a bag of marshmallows. At times like this, he needed something to chew and marshmallows were quieter than crisps.

'Bugsy, do you reckon this is another no-show?'

'Looks like it, Jack. Mind you, after that poor sod in North Shields, we can't be sure. Our killer could turn up anywhere.'

'Why do you suppose he travelled all that way, just to kill a fishmonger who'd once been a goalkeeper for Richington United's football team? It doesn't make any sense.'

'If we're expecting any of these murders to make sense, I reckon we'll be disappointed, guv. I mean, murder's never right, is it? But at least with some that we've handled, you could see why it happened. When the killer just picks 'em off a photograph at random, like this, it makes it much harder to catch the bugger.'

'Is it random, though, Bugsy? My copper's nose tells me that there's something else behind this. Something darker and deeper.'

* * *

By Friday, with no murders having been reported for two months, the *Echo*, it seemed, had lost interest in the Moon Killer and had moved on to more important issues, such as the scandalous state of the Kings Richington public toilets. Jack called the team together to discuss their next move. They were seated around the big, oval table in the incident room and he was about to begin when the door opened. It was Professor Davenport.

'I hope it's OK, Jack. I thought I'd call in just to check that you and Corrie are still on for Saturday evening.'

'Absolutely. It's good to see you, Cressida. How are you feeling?'

She looked pale still, but it was only a month or so since her operation, and Corrie had said it would take her some time to recover properly. 'Oh, I'm getting there, thanks. A couple more weeks and they think I should be able to go back to work. I'm not interrupting, am I?'

'No, we were about to discuss why our killer appears to have stopped killing. Every full moon for five months and now nothing for the last two. Should we still be on high alert? We'd be interested in your views.'

She sat down at the table and Simon fetched her a cup of coffee. 'Could be any number of reasons. Kings Richington has been swarming with detectives and men in uniform. If he's a local man, and we believe he is, he'll have seen that and maybe decided it's too risky at the moment. He may even have come close to capture, so he's decided to keep a low profile. For example, the first four victims weren't found until he was well clear. The last two you had identified and warned, yet he still went ahead and risked being caught.'

'Or he could have just run out of victims,' offered Bugsy. 'That's my theory. I think he's waiting for us to find them for him, from that photograph.'

Cressida shook her head. 'No, I don't think so, Sergeant. His profile suggests a deep-seated need to kill and I'm sure he would have continued until we stopped him, had he been able. Of course, he could be lying in hospital somewhere after a terrible accident or with some life-threatening disease. And here's something you might not have considered — he might already be in custody for some unrelated crime. Something less serious. He'll continue with his real quest when he comes out.'

'Are you saying that once he's killed all the young men in that football photo, he'll stop?' asked Simon.

'No, not at all. That appears to be his focus at the moment, we have no idea why. And he may not be planning to kill them all. He's very likely, in my judgement, to move on to other groups, such as masons, doctors, or even,' she smiled, 'dare I say, policemen? We mustn't become too hung up on footballers, or we could lose sight of the bigger picture.'

'And what is the bigger picture, Professor?' asked Aled.

'This type of serial killer feels a need, almost a duty, to kill certain types of people. He may even hear voices or see visions compelling him to do it. We have to be prepared to act when he starts on a different category of victim.'

'Let's hope it isn't coppers', muttered Bugsy. 'There aren't enough of us as it is.'

Jack looked pensive. 'Sergeant, I believe you've just given me an idea.'

'What's that, guv?' Bugsy was surprised. It wasn't often he gave anyone ideas.

'I don't want to let the cat out of the bag just yet. Not until I've thought it through. And it's a pretty big cat . . . I doubt I'd be able to cram it back in.'

CHAPTER TWENTY-TWO

'Jack, can you pass me that gizmo, please?' Corrie was packing food, dishes and utensils into large containers, ready to take to the Davenports for dinner that evening. All the meals from Coriander's Cuisine were excellent, she made sure of that. Quality control was of the utmost importance. It was quality that ensured customers came back and recommended her to their friends. But this one was special. Cressida had been through a major operation and Corrie wanted it to be particularly special for her.

Jack picked up the 'gizmo.' 'What is this?'

'It's what ladies use when there isn't a man available.'

He turned it over in his hand, puzzled. 'Where do you put the batteries?'

Corrie looked at him. 'It doesn't have batteries you push it over the top and twist.' She saw his startled expression. 'Jack, for goodness' sake! It's a gadget for taking the tops off bottles. I need it in case the caps on the wine bottles are tight and I can't unscrew them. I can hardly bring them into the dining room and ask one of the men to do it, can I?'

'I doubt if Cressida would need it. She probably rips them off with her teeth.'

'That's very unkind. She has . . . well . . . muscles, that's all.'

'You're telling me. The first time she shook my hand, it took me ten minutes to get the blood back into my fingers.'

'Oliver's ripped, too. You can see his muscle definition through his shirt.'

'Ripped?' said Jack. 'Since when did you start using words like that?'

'It's what Carlene said about that constable in your office.'

Jack sighed. 'You'll be getting tattoos next.'

* * *

Corrie thought the dinner was going extremely well, even if she did say it herself. There were twelve seated around the beautiful, oak dining table, all expensively suited and booted. Cressida had chosen a seafood platter to start, followed by Beef Wellington — always a showstopping centrepiece on a special occasion. Corrie thought Cressida looked fragile and pale, despite the make-up that she had expertly applied in an attempt to give herself some colour. Oliver was particularly solicitous and wouldn't even let her lift the serving dishes.

Everyone ate with gusto and at the end of the meal there was a relaxed, postprandial hum of banking talk. Once they started mentioning annual percentage yields and closed-end loans, Cressida called a halt.

She stood up. 'Ladies, shall we repair to the kitchen for coffee and gossip?'

After the usual discussions about the best hairdressers in town, the latest films you shouldn't miss and the appalling one-way traffic system if you were coming down the High Street in anything bigger than a mini, conversation turned to the Moon Killer. With Corrie being the wife of the Senior Investigating Officer, and Cressida the criminal profiler, questions were inevitable.

'Can we assume we're safe now, Mrs Dawes?' asked a lady with vivid orange hair. 'After all, there hasn't been a murder since August.'

Corrie shrugged. 'I really don't know. All I can say is that the police are continuing to work tirelessly, following up every lead, in order to bring this man to justice. He's killed six people. Even if he doesn't kill again, he mustn't be allowed to remain at liberty.' *Here I go again*, she thought. *An unofficial police spokesperson, spouting the official line-to-take. I should get paid for this.*

'I agree,' added Cressida. 'And we don't know how many others he's killed that the police don't even know about yet. In my experience, cases like this are rarely clear-cut. The killer, as a child, will have demonstrated warning behaviours such as bedwetting, cruelty to animals and starting fires. These can typically spiral into murder.'

Corrie thought this a strange observation. Jack hadn't mentioned further victims or that they didn't know where some of the bodies were buried. She was sure he was focused on the lads in the football team.

'Do you think he'll start killing women?' asked a rather nervous-looking lady.

Cressida nodded. 'Very possibly. His criminal profile indicates that events in his past could easily trigger a vendetta against women. In his disturbed mind, he'll be punishing all the women who have let him down in the past, from his mother not breastfeeding him, to a random checkout girl who short-changed him.'

'Christ! None of us is safe,' declared someone else. 'So you're saying if I carved him up at a roundabout, I could be on his list?'

'Yep. He'll have taken your registration number,' joked Cressida. 'And now I think I need to 'fess up.'

Whatever's coming now? wondered Corrie. *She's already put the wind up everyone.*

'The magnificent meal that we've all enjoyed was not my creation. It was from Coriander's Cuisine.' She gestured at Corrie. There was a rather rowdy round of applause and alcohol-induced cheering. 'I'm sure Corrie has some of her business cards with her, and you'll all want to take one and use her services for your next dinner party.'

* * *

Several miles away, in a kitchen very different to the Davenports', Iris was making Bugsy a late supper of cheese on toast after the theatre.

'I know you've been busy with this awful serial killer investigation, Mike, but is there a chance you might get some time off later in the year? If he doesn't strike again, I mean.'

'I expect so.' Bugsy had cut his slice of toasted cheese into four pieces with a knife, rather than picking it up whole and biting lumps off, like he usually did. He had also tucked his napkin into his collar. That way, he could stop the grease from the cheese from running down his shirt. 'Why, what were you thinking?'

'I know Christmas is a few weeks away yet, but I thought I'd get in early, before you made other plans.'

Bugsy never made any plans for Christmas. It was always the same. He volunteered to go into work, so the young blokes with kids could have time off. Then he came home, heated up the turkey dinner with all the trimmings that Mrs D always gave him and watched crap on telly until he fell asleep.

Iris was tentative. 'I wondered whether you might like to spend next Christmas with us — that's me, Dan, Cheryl and the grandchildren. I warn you, it'll be totally manic. We play daft games, pull crackers and stuff ourselves stupid. Please don't be afraid to say if you'd rather not. I won't mind.'

But Bugsy could see that she would mind, very much. And he really couldn't believe his luck. 'I'd love to, Iris, but you have to understand, I haven't spent Christmas with a proper family since I was a boy. You'd have to promise to tell me if I wasn't doing it right. I mean, I might get them all the wrong presents and I can't sing carols in tune to save me life . . . '

Iris put her arms around him. 'You'll be lovely, like you always are. You couldn't be anything else.' She gave him a kiss.

When he got home, Bugsy poured himself a nightcap. Who'd have thought it? He was actually looking forward to Christmas. He was usually glad when it was over. *The Moon Killer had better not spoil it*, he thought. *Or I'll wring the bastard's neck myself!*

It almost came to that.

CHAPTER TWENTY-THREE

Halloween came and went amid a massive demand in Corrie's Kitchen for party food. Eyeball lollipops, spider's web cakes and kiwi slime pies flew from the kitchen to the delivery vans. Bonfire night was much the same. A variety of different hot dogs, baked potatoes and Catherine wheel Cumberland sausages were packed in cartons shaped like picnic baskets for people to take with them to firework displays. Inspector Dawes and his team were on duty, supporting a busy fire brigade in an attempt to keep everyone safe.

Oliver and Cressida Davenport were back training again, building up their strength after over two months of inactivity. Oliver was weight training and Cressida was in her Krav Maga class. She had wondered whether she would still have the necessary stamina, but after she successfully attacked and overcame her instructor four out of five times, she was starting to believe in herself again.

Cressida liked all forms of contact combat, but Krav Maga was different. It was originally an Israeli army self-defence technique, designed for street fighting, but it had become popular with women who, on average, have a size and strength disadvantage in combat. The moves are fast and explosive, involving brutal attacks on the body's vulnerable points, viciously executed, as if in a life-and-death situation. There are no sporting rules and no let-up until the opponent is incapacitated. Cressida made for the showers, pleased with her performance. As her instructor had pointed out, there are no superior styles, only superior practitioners.

* * *

Before the next full moon in November, Jack called his core team together for a meeting. He wanted to put an idea to them. It was something that had been buzzing around in his head since Professor Davenport had expressed the possibility that the serial killer could move on to another group of professionals. Bugsy had said he hoped it wouldn't be coppers. *But why not?* Jack had thought. *Why not use that to our advantage?*

The troops gathered round after hours, fortified with pizzas from Corrie's Kitchen. Jack had asked Professor Davenport to join them. Her opinion would be informed by psychology, and therefore useful.

'There's going to be another full moon very soon.' There were groans. Jack carried on. 'We've no way of knowing if our serial killer is going to strike again, but how about we start to be proactive this time, instead of reactive?'

'How do you mean, sir?' asked Aled.

'We let it be known, covertly of course, that we've identified another of the footballers from the photo.'

'Have we?' asked Cressida.

'No, but we'll put the word in a few ears — bent journalists, police informers, rough pubs and clubs, everywhere that criminal low life congregates. We'll make it clear that this is top secret information, knowing that these are the people who are least likely to keep it to themselves. By the time we get to full moon, half of Kings Richington will know about it. Hopefully, that will include our killer. Given that he's been unable, for whatever reason, to release that built-up tension that the professor's been telling us about, he'll be unable to resist the opportunity for gratification.'

'OK, guv, with you so far,' said Bugsy. 'How's that going to help us catch him? Are you planning to set a trap and get one of the lads from Richington United to be the bait?'

'Yes and no, Sergeant. I'm planning to set a trap, but not with a footballer. That would be too dangerous, and they're all too young. This man would need to be around forty, like the others. In any case, we can't put a member of the public at risk. But we could use a police volunteer.'

The room went quiet while the team took this on board. Jack continued to explain the next part of his strategy. 'We quietly foster the story that, having identified this man, we're keeping him in a safe house until we've caught the killer. We'll give him a name, preferably one of the real Under-21s who were around at that time. I was thinking Bert Roberts might be able to remember one of his son's random teammates, even if he wasn't in the photograph. On the day of the full moon, we'll have all available officers in parked cars, close by the safe house and in full radio contact. Then, when the killer strikes, as I'm pretty sure he will, we grab him. What do you say?'

'Good idea, sir. I reckon it could work,' said Aled. 'Catch him off guard instead of letting him make fools of us again.'

'Who's going to do it, sir?' asked Simon.

'It would have to be a volunteer, as I said. I can't assign someone.'

'I'll do it, Jack,' said Bugsy, immediately.

Good old Bugsy, thought Jack. *Always the first to volunteer without any consideration of the danger.* 'Sorry, Sergeant Malone, but like me you're a couple of years too old.'

'I'll do it, sir,' chorused Aled and Simon.

'And you guys are too young, and before you put your hand up, Gemma, you'd never get away with it, not even in a boiler suit with a bag over your head.'

Silence. DC Mitchell coughed. 'Looks like it's down to me, then, sir.'

'Only if you're sure, Mitch. I won't lie, it's not without a fair degree of risk, but I promise we'll minimize that risk by having every angle covered. Take some time to think it over before you decide.'

'I don't need to, sir. We've got to stop this man somehow, and my military training will come in useful when he goes for me.'

Jack was glad Mitch had volunteered. He was ex-SAS and the least vulnerable in a combat situation. He was around forty, the right age, and had kept in shape.

Professor Davenport had stayed very quiet until now. 'Won't that make Mitch an *agent provocateur*, Jack?'

'Very probably,' agreed Jack. 'Quite honestly, in view of the number of murders our man has committed, I don't think any jury would care how we catch him, only that we do. The imperative is to stop the blighter. I'll argue the legality of it afterwards.'

Cressida frowned. 'There's another thing that occurs to me. What if he's already planned his next victim? Another of the real faces from the photograph. While Mitch is tethered to the post, the tiger could be hunting in a different part of the jungle entirely.'

'I take your point, Cressida, but if we throw out the challenge cleverly enough, I don't think he'll be able to resist. He'll want to show he's smarter than the police, and he'll think he can always pick off the other target next time.'

'If Mitch is up for it, I think we should do it, guv,' said Bugsy. There were nods of agreement from the rest of the team. 'Maybe we shouldn't tell the chief super until afterwards, though. He's on leave for a couple of weeks. It'll all be over by the time he comes back.'

'Good thinking.' If Garwood knew what he was planning, he'd self-combust. In his absence, Jack had the freedom to deploy resources however he thought fit. 'Now we've decided to go ahead, it's imperative that the real purpose of the plan should be kept on a need-to-know basis. If the killer gets wind that it's a set-up, the whole thing will be an expensive waste of time.'

'Let's call it Operation Moonshine,' suggested Gemma.

'Good idea, Gemma. That's how we'll refer to it from now on. We'll use this end-of-terrace safe house on the far edge of town.' Jack pointed to it on the map. Now that the concept had been agreed, he was on to the practicalities.

'Is that the one where we put that bank guard last year?' asked Bugsy. 'He witnessed a vicious armed robbery and a bank security guard was shot. We had the gang in custody, awaiting trial.'

'That's the one. The gang's contacts on the outside swore they'd get him before the trial, but they didn't. The house is bristling with alarm systems that feed straight through to the station. There are loads of places to conceal officers in cars and plenty of CCTV outside. Mitch will be wired up, of course. Can we do it with Wi-Fi, Clive?'

'I'm sure we can, sir. I'll investigate the systems.'

'Are you planning on putting another officer in there with Mitch, sir?' asked Gemma. 'I could do that. I could pretend to be his wife.'

'Thanks, Gemma, but I'd rather do this alone,' said Mitch. 'If I was really in danger of being topped, I wouldn't want my wife at risk, would I?'

'No, I suppose not.'

'And we'll need to maintain radio silence unless it's an emergency,' added Clive. 'This bloke's clever. He's almost certainly able to tune in to the police network.'

'That's fine with me,' said Mitch. 'As soon as I've got the bloke, I'll raise the alarm.'

'Hopefully,' said Sergeant Parsloe, 'we'll have spotted him before he gets to you, and uniform will take him out.'

'We need to talk about dates,' said Jack. 'Clive, you're the amateur astronomer among us. Tell us when we should activate Operation Moonshine.' Clive was an undoubted nerd, but sometimes, a nerd was what you needed.

Clive looked at the notes on his laptop. 'The Beaver Moon, sometimes called the Frost or Snow Moon, reaches peak illumination in the UK at 1:34 p.m. on Tuesday the twelfth of November. NASA is quite excited about this one,

140

expecting a spectacular brightness. However, it can appear full for around three days. For example, on the eleventh of November, it might appear full, but then it's a Waxing Gibbous moon and only ninety-nine per cent bright.'

'We don't really know what it is about the lunar phases that triggers the killer, do we?' Gemma asked.

'Quite right,' agreed Professor Davenport. 'When will you install Mitch in the safe house, Jack?'

'I think, in order to give us the best chance of success, he should go in on Monday the eleventh of November and stay there until close of play on Wednesday the thirteenth. Officers outside will work on a shift basis so that there are always enough cars on duty. If the killer hasn't struck by Wednesday night, I think we can take it that he isn't going to and that it is, finally, the end of the Moon Killer. In the meantime, it's another waiting game, I'm afraid.'

'We could look at some of the unanswered questions from the previous six killings. They could help with planning the trap,' suggested Simon. 'For example, should we consider that it was the killer who went into the Chinese takeaway looking for Walker, then when he didn't find him, he telephoned Walker's employer for a forwarding address, pretending to be the police?'

'I don't see who else it could have been,' offered Aled.

'Can we really not get any kind of number from a burner phone?' asked Simon.

'Apparently not,' said Jack. 'The techies were on it for weeks. If you buy a pay-as-you-go phone, use it once, then turn it off, it's impossible to trace. You can take out the SIM card and battery and chuck the whole lot in the river, it makes no difference. Once the phone's off, everything is dead. It can't communicate with cell towers. It can only be traced to the location it was in when it was powered down. GPS is no help, as it needs consistent cellular or internet access to gather location details.'

'Do we think that's what the Moon Killer did?' asked Bugsy.

'Something of the sort. In any event, we weren't able to get any kind of information from Richington United because their telephone system didn't record a number. Clive, you've worked on whether we can get a fix on a burner phone that's been switched off. We can't do it, can we?'

'NASA claim they can, sir, even when the phone is turned off, but they don't want to explain how. I reckon they must infect the handsets with Trojans which would force them to continue emitting a signal. It wouldn't work if the battery was removed, though, as the phone wouldn't have a power source to send signals and would fail to share its location details. I could message them if you like.'

'I doubt if NASA would be interested in helping with our problem, but thanks anyway.'

'One thing that's been worrying me,' said Aled, 'is how did the killer find Joe Roberts? The other five victims were pretty much local. According to the statement we took from Bert Roberts, the family moved to North Shields when Joe was offered a job with Newcastle United.'

'That's pretty easy these days,' offered Gemma. She wasn't the most outspoken officer on his team, but Jack always knew that when she did speak, it would be useful. 'There are plenty of sites for finding people on the internet if you know where to look. I tried it, sir. Google was my first port of call, in case Roberts was on a public website somewhere. Look what I found.'

She turned her laptop around so they could all see. There, on Facebook, was a photo of the late Joe Roberts. His profile had full details of his training with the Richington United Under-21 football team and the subsequent trial he'd had with Newcastle some twenty years ago, he'd been so proud of it. Later posts advertised his fish shop on the Fish Quay in North Shields. There was even a map.

'Thanks, Gemma,' said Jack. 'That's cleared that up. Couldn't have been easier for the killer to find him, could it?'

* * *

Jack was interested to see that now she had recovered, Professor Davenport made frequent visits to the incident room to liaise with the team on Operation Moonshine. She maintained her previous stance that this man would have continued to kill until he was stopped. However, he had stopped after August, when he had killed Vic Walker. Who or what had stopped him, they had yet to discover.

She suggested a trawl of local hospitals, both medical and mental, to enquire if they had recently admitted any long-stay patients. Also, an examination of deaths registered between 15 August — the last murder — and 14 September, when they had expected another. Their man could have died of something rapid, like sepsis, or been run over by a bus.

These activities were labour-intensive and, in Jack's view, a waste of time, but he reluctantly provided the resources on the understanding that it would be all hands to Operation Moonshine when the time came.

CHAPTER TWENTY-FOUR

November 12. The Beaver Moon

The safe house was stocked with food, utilities had been switched on and the alarm technology had been activated and tested. Mitch was wired up with a tiny but effective microphone and transmitter underneath his shirt. They moved him in on Monday 11 November at 9 a.m.

There were eight cars parked outside — two in the road at the back of the house, one directly opposite in the drive of a bungalow belonging to a curious but cooperative lady, and the rest at intervals to the left and right of the property. They were all anonymous, unremarkable looking cars of different makes and sizes. Bugsy and Aled took first shift in the road at the back, with Jack and Simon waiting to take over. Gemma Fox and Norman Parsloe sat in the drive opposite. More plain clothes officers from the MIT occupied the other cars.

Inside the house, Mitch was reading the paper but was on high alert for anything out of the ordinary. They had parked a car from the police pool in the drive outside. It would have been unreasonable not to provide the man in the safe house with some means of transport in case a fast getaway became necessary. Particularly when his life was in danger. Operation Moonshine was underway.

* * *

DS Malone had contacted DS Billy Purvis in North Shields. A chat with Bert Roberts had provided the name of one of Joe's teammates to use as Mitch's false footballer identity. Johnnie Johnson had been a close friend but had never made the team and had since transferred his attention to engineering. He was now a welder in Sheffield.

The Kings Richington grapevine worked like magic. The intelligence that a potential Moon Killer victim had been located and put in a safe house spread like wildfire. The more people who were told it was confidential for the safety of Johnnie Johnson, the more they passed it on. The criminal underbelly of Kings Richington, which is where Jack suspected the Moon Killer was sheltering, was positively ecstatic, believing they now had access to secret police information. What other useful intelligence might they learn?

By nightfall, nothing had happened. Mitch had cooked himself some food, watched television and now lay on the bed, fully clothed, with the lights out and curtains drawn. Outside, Jack and Simon were drinking coffee from a flask and eating sandwiches that Corrie had provided.

PC Jackson was pleased to be part of a covert operation and at doing his first stint on 'obbo.' It would be useful experience for his fast track assessment. He looked out of the window at the sky. The Waxing Gibbous moon was bright but not entirely full yet.

'So that's a Beaver Moon, sir. NASA was right, it is rather stunning.'

'Let's hope our killer thinks so and is induced to chance his arm,' said Jack. 'Our goat is tethered, Simon, now where's the tiger?'

* * *

Professor Davenport had told Jack that she didn't think there would be any particular advantage in her becoming involved in the activities of Operation Moonshine at ground level. He'd agreed but suggested she might like to be present when they interviewed the killer, as she may well want to appear as an expert witness at his trial. She had to admire Jack's optimism, however misplaced, and had agreed to that. She discussed it with Oliver when she got home that night.

'Do you think this serial killer will take the bait?' he asked.

'Not really,' she said. 'I think he's too smart.'

'He must be very smart to have outwitted the police all this time,' agreed Oliver. 'They're no closer to catching him now than they were back in March.'

'On the other hand, if he really wants to show the police how inept they are, like Jack the Ripper did, he may have a go, right under their noses, just for the hell of it.'

'True,' said Oliver. 'After all, he hasn't killed since August. He might be having withdrawal symptoms.'

She laughed. 'Can you have withdrawal symptoms from giving up murdering people?'

'If it's an addiction, like smoking, I'm sure you can. But you're the psychologist, darling. You tell me.'

* * *

At precisely 1:34 p.m. on Tuesday 12 November, the Beaver Moon reached peak illumination. Outside the safe house, the officers in the cars were none the wiser, as it was covered in dense cloud and pouring with rain. They sat on guard for the rest of the day until the night shift took over. There were still thick clouds and the rain was emptying down, so nobody, apart from possibly NASA, saw anything of the moon at all.

That evening, Mitch Mitchell, aka Johnnie Johnson, had finished his lasagne supper and was dozing, with one eye open, in an armchair. The silence was broken by a loud rattle, then a crash in the kitchen. Someone had knocked something over in the dark. Mitch went into commando mode.

He switched off the table lamp and whispered 'Moonshine! Moonshine!' into his microphone — the agreed code call for assistance. He kicked open the kitchen door and pounced on the first thing that moved.

Officers broke cover and streamed up to the house from all directions, shouting to each other. Before any of them had reached the door, Mitch transmitted again.

'It's all right. Stand down. It's a cat, come inside out of the rain. Nobody told me there was a cat flap in the back door. The poor thing's soaked.'

'So are we now, Mitch,' complained Bugsy. 'Thanks a million.'

* * *

Wednesday 13 November was the last day of Operation Moonshine, which was looking like a total washout, both functionally and meteorologically. By the afternoon, Bugsy and Aled had run out of diversions and agreed there was a limit to how many games of 'I spy' you could play without getting on each other's nerves.

'Bugger this for a game of soldiers.' Bugsy had finished the flask of soup that Iris had given him and eaten both his pork pies. 'I could murder some fish and chips. What about you, Taffy?'

'I don't suppose it'll do any harm if we just drive around the corner to the chippy, Sarge. We'll only be gone ten minutes.'

Their car was the only one in plain sight of the side gate, which was concealed by a large pine tree and therefore not covered by the CCTV. As Bugsy said afterwards, without a degree in geometry to work out the angles and ratios, there was really no way they could have known this.

* * *

At midnight, Jack decided to stand the team down. He lifted radio silence and spoke to them.

'Well, Operation Moonshine, the good news is that it looks like the plague of murders is finally at an end. If the Moon Killer was still active, he wouldn't have been able to resist turning up at some point over the last three days. The bad news is we still haven't caught him. I'd like to know what stopped him, but I suppose we should just be thankful that something did. Thanks very much, everyone. Safe home and get some sleep. You too, Mitch, and thanks for your help.'

One by one, the observation cars made their way down the tree-lined avenue and across Kings Richington back to their homes. Inside the safe house, Mitch took off his shirt, removed the radio transmitter and microphone and stashed them in his bag. He pulled on a hoodie, gathered his belongings, fed the cat and turned out the lights. Outside in the drive, he threw his backpack into the boot of the car and climbed into the driving seat. He didn't know whether he was glad or disappointed that he hadn't come face to face with his quarry.

Before he could start the engine, cupped hands clapped hard over his ears. The impact deafened him. He was disorientated, but he knew there was someone in the back seat. In the moments that he was struggling with shock and pain, a hand came over his shoulder and grabbed his head. Gloved fingers rammed into his open mouth. The other hand grasped the back of his skull and twisted with a violent jerk.

* * *

At half past midnight, there was a 999 call from the lady who lived in the bungalow opposite the safe house.

'Hello. Is that the police?' She gave them her name, address and phone number. 'I've been watching the police operations across the road from my bedroom window. All your officers have left now, but the man who has been living in the house opposite for the last three days is still here. I was worried because I saw him come out half an hour ago and get into his car. I couldn't see very well because there's a tree in the way, but I think there was someone in the back seat. It looked like there was a struggle, then whoever was in the back jumped out and ran off. Your man is still there, in his car. He isn't moving. Could you send someone, please?'

DI Dawes was on the scene in ten minutes. DS Malone was close behind. The area car was already there and they had called an ambulance. DC Mitchell was lying across the seat.

They hadn't dared to move him. He was still alive, but only just.

'Hang on, Mitch,' begged Jack, though Mitch couldn't hear him. 'The ambulance is on its way. Don't try to talk.'

The paramedics went straight into action. They examined Mitch, gave him oxygen, applied a neck support and bandaged his head. He was bleeding from both ears and his mouth. They set up a drip, stretchered him into the ambulance and sped away with sirens and lights blaring.

Jack was stunned. 'My God, Bugsy, how could this have happened? We carried out every possible risk assessment. I promised Mitch that nothing would happen to him.'

Bugsy was angry. 'The bastard must have somehow crept through that side gate and into his car. Then he waited until we'd all gone and Mitch came out to drive home. Why didn't Mitch leave at the same time as the rest of us, guv?'

'I'll bet he stopped to feed that bloody cat. But given the high level of surveillance we set up, why didn't somebody see the killer getting in through the side gate? We had "eyeballs" on all the entrances — I made sure of it. Clive did drawings and calculations to make sure there were no blind spots. We even had a sketch map.'

Then Bugsy remembered. He and Williams had left their post and gone to get fish and chips. 'Jack, I think this is my fault.'

CHAPTER TWENTY-FIVE

Dawes and Malone raced to the hospital, blues and twos full on. The doctor was waiting to speak to them.

'DC Mitchell was able to explain a little of what happened to him, but he's now sedated. Someone clapped his ears, violently, from behind. The vibrations have caused both ear drums to perforate and he could have internal bleeding in his brain. We'll need a scan to see how bad that might be. In addition, his head has been twisted round violently and the jerk may have fractured some vertebrae, or, worst case scenario, damaged his spinal cord. We'll know more after he's strong enough to undergo some tests. He said he didn't see who it was, but the assailant was extremely strong. He said to tell you he's sorry he didn't get him.'

'Did you find anything down his throat, Doctor?' asked Jack.

The doctor looked puzzled. 'No, there was nothing in his throat, Inspector.'

Thank God, thought Jack. *If there had been, Mitch would most likely be dead.*

* * *

Back in the car they sat stunned, praying that Mitch would recover. If he did, Jack would make it his business to see he got a commendation.

'It was him, wasn't it, Jack?' said Bugsy. 'The bastard's laughing at us. Somehow, he knew that Mitch wasn't Johnnie Johnson, the footballer, that's why he didn't kill him outright and stick a tampon down his throat. He's showing us he could have, if he'd wanted to.'

'That means someone on the team leaked the information,' said Jack. 'Nobody outside of Operation Moonshine knew it wasn't genuine. I didn't even tell Corrie. Apart from us, everybody else involved in setting up the safe house believed it was a victim protection case.'

Bugsy shook his head. 'I can't believe any of the team would do that, Jack. They're all totally committed to catching this lunatic.'

'I agree. It proves one thing, though. Professor Davenport was wrong about his profile suggesting a deep-seated need to kill, indiscriminately if necessary. If that had been the case, he'd have killed Mitch when he had the chance. No, I believe he has a very specific motive.'

'But we still don't have a clear idea what that motive is.'

* * *

DC Williams and DC Fox visited the lady who had made the 999 call. She couldn't add much to what she had already told them, except she was sure the figure who got out of the back of the car was dressed all in black, including something over the head. No, she couldn't tell whether it was a man or a woman, but she thought probably a man because he was tall. They took her statement and thanked her. It may well have been her vigilance that saved DC Mitchell's life.

* * *

When Chief Superintendent Garwood returned from leave some two weeks later, DI Dawes filled him in on what had happened. Jack thought he'd have apoplexy, he went such an unhealthy colour.

'You did what, Dawes? Three days of staking out a safe house and one officer down?'

'DC Mitchell is recovering well, sir. Thankfully, there shouldn't be any lasting damage, according to the hospital.'

'What did you think you were doing, man?'

'I knew you wouldn't want us to ease up on trying to hunt this killer down. Now for the first time, we have a live victim of an attack. Our six murders are rapidly becoming cold cases and I'm sure you won't want that on your record for the remainder of your service, sir.'

'Certainly not, Dawes.' That was the last thing Garwood wanted. He planned to go out with a knighthood. 'Stay with it, man. Use whatever resources you need. Keep me informed.'

* * *

Christmas was rapidly approaching, and the stores in Kings Richington High Street had been displaying trees, baubles and lights since October. The customary twenty-metre Christmas tree had been installed in the town square and the lights had been switched on by a local celebrity — a minor soap star that no one had heard of — but it was all very festive and everyone enjoyed it.

That evening, Iris and Bugsy were strolling through town admiring the street lamps decorated with bells, snow-men and candles. Kings Richington's various clubs and commercial enterprises always made a good effort. Every shop boasted a tree with lights and snowflakes on the windows. There was Christmas music and groups of carol singers with lanterns gathered at intervals along the high street.

'Don't you just love Christmas, Mike? It's so full of hope and excitement. It's my favourite time of year.'

Bugsy squeezed her hand. 'To be honest, Iris, it didn't mean a lot to me, not until I met you. Now it's my favourite time, too.'

'Oh look! The German Christmas market's set up over there. Shall we have gluhwein?'

Bugsy had never tasted gluhwein, but his life now was full of new experiences. 'Yes, of course, if you'd like some.'

They sat at one of the little rustic tables with checked tablecloths. Bugsy bought big wedges of apple strudel to go with the gluhwein. He thought it all tasted wonderful, but it may have been the company. He had never believed he would find such happiness at his time of life. Right now, the horrors of the Moon Killer seemed a long way off.

'What are you doing on Thursday, Mike?'

'Working as usual. Why, what would you like me to do?'

'Dan and Cheryl have received a complimentary voucher from Hambridges department store. It's for Christmas lunch in the restaurant. Dan has taken a day off from the surgery so we could all go. He doesn't get much time off at this time of year. Everyone has coughs, colds and flu. I spend all my time on reception trying to persuade them that the best treatment for a common cold is to stay home and rest with warm drinks and over the counter remedies to soothe their symptoms. But they insist on seeing the doctor, convinced if they don't get antibiotics, they'll drop dead. The men are the worst.'

Bugsy thought he might have had man flu once or twice but funnily enough, it always seemed to disappear once he got to the station and had some breakfast in the canteen. He thought it had something to do with there being no one at home to pamper him so he was better off at work.

Iris sipped her second gluhwein. Her cheeks were taking on a rosy glow, despite the cold. 'I've taken the day off too, so we thought we'd all come into town, have lunch out, and look around Hambridges. We might see something for the grandchildren. The toy department is huge and they have a lovely Santa's grotto.'

Hambridges was a big department store that dominated Kings Richington High Street. At Christmas, they took great pride in their animated window display. Each year it took on a different theme that was revealed to the public early in November. This year, it featured a snow scene with Santa's sleigh soaring up into the sky pulled by galloping reindeer. Down below, there was a toy workshop with elves busily making all kinds of toys — traditional toys, not games consoles and tablets. It was magical. Children would stand staring at it, spellbound.

'Do you think you'd be able to come, Mike? It would be such fun and the children would love it if you were there too.'

Bugsy had a vague recollection that Thursday was the next full moon, but there hadn't been a murder since August and mercifully, the attack on DC Mitchell hadn't proved fatal. In fact, he'd been discharged from hospital and had come into the station wearing a neck support, to prove it would take more than a deranged psychopath to shut him down. His hearing was starting to return, and in the meantime, everybody was happy to shout.

Bugsy didn't imagine there would be a problem with him taking the day off. 'I'll speak to Jack, but I'm sure it'll be OK. Thank you for inviting me, Iris.'

When he dropped her outside her house, she took his face in her hands and gave him a proper kiss. He kissed her back. As he walked to his car, he wanted to do that thing where you jump in the air and click your heels together. He didn't because he thought he might do himself a mischief. But he was doing it in his head, which was almost as good.

* * *

When Bugsy arrived at the station next morning, he looked at the full moon schedule that DC Williams had pinned to the whiteboard. The next full moon, the last one of the year, was on 12 December at 12:12 a.m. It was called the Cold

Moon. Bugsy thought that's exactly what it would be at that time in the morning. Snow was forecast. He reckoned it should be called the Bloody Cold Moon. He'd come in via the canteen and was carrying two coffees and two mince pies. He put a coffee and a pie on Jack's desk and sat down.

'Morning, Jack. What are the chances of me having Thursday off?'

'Morning, Bugsy. I don't see why not.' He sipped the scalding coffee.

'Only it is a full moon.' He pointed to the board. 'Mind you, after the cock-up I made at the November one, I might be better off out of the way.'

'There are plenty of us here to cover if something does kick off. But I don't think it will, somehow. I know the professor still insists that this man will carry on killing. She believes he's been stopped by something beyond his control and he'll find his next victim when he's able.'

'But you're not so sure?' asked Bugsy.

Jack was thoughtful. 'No, I think this is the end of it. I think he set out to kill a precise number of men, for a specific reason. I don't believe it's indiscriminate, even if we haven't been able to find the motive. He's stopped because he's satisfied that he's got them all. The attack on Mitch was just muscle flexing, to give us a metaphorical kick up the arse.'

* * *

That night when he got home, Jack just had to tell Corrie about Bugsy's intended Christmas shopping trip with Iris and her family. He couldn't believe the transformation that had come over his old friend and colleague. Maybe there was something in this online dating after all.

'Apparently, Iris's son has been sent some sort of gift voucher from Hambridges for complimentary lunch, then they're going to visit Santa's grotto with the kids. Iris has invited Bugsy to go with them.'

'I think that's lovely. Christmas is the time for family and I'm so glad Bugsy has found a good one. He's been on his own far too long.'

Jack looked pensive. 'Do you wish we had a family to spend Christmas with?'

Corrie grinned. 'Definitely not, sweetheart. By the time we get to Christmas Eve and I've delivered twenty billion turkey dinners, never mind all the puddings, mince pies and vegan stuff, I'm hoping to be ding dong merrily on high!'

CHAPTER TWENTY-SIX

12 December. The Cold Moon

Coriander's Cuisine was always busy at Christmas, but this year, it was frenzied. Corrie had taken on extra staff to cope with the pressure. The businesswoman in her did not like to turn away customers. It seemed that the party season was set to last from the beginning of December until well into the New Year.

The great and the good of Kings Richington had unanimously decided that having Christmas delivered was a better option than cooking it yourself. As one client had observed to Corrie, '*What's the point of buying food if you have to fiddle with it when you get it home?*' Even Corrie's Kitchen was inundated with requests for quick party food that you could eat with your fingers while you were dancing. This was something of a challenge, especially as Corrie wasn't au fait with modern dance styles. Mini sausage rolls were probably a safe bet, but boring and could get flaky in a salsa situation. Saucy Spanish meatballs were popular but messy.

The outside door flew open and Carlene tottered in carrying several trays of mince pies, piled in a precarious tower. Her hair was escaping from under her cap and her whites were limp with the heat from the ovens. She put the mince pies down carefully and stopped to catch her breath.

'Blimey, Mrs D, it's like "Bake Off" on speed in there!'

Corrie laughed. 'I know. Are they coping all right?'

'Oh yeah. As long as they've got Michael Bublé coming through the speakers, they're happy.'

'Carlene, you're familiar with the club scene. What finger food can we provide for people to eat while they're capering about?'

'Well, my friend Antoine, who's a sous chef at Le Canard Bleu in town, gets bits of Caesar chicken and prawns wrapped in bread, stuff like that, then he kebabs 'em on little cocktail sticks. People just grab one as they boogie past. The clever part is that you can bung it in your mouth in one go, chuck the stick away, and your fingers don't get messy.'

'That sounds great.' Corrie was thinking more about how pleased she was that Carlene had a boyfriend, especially one who worked in a posh French restaurant. The mini kebab idea was good, too.

Carlene picked up an order sheet. 'This one came in a bit late last night, didn't it? A romantic meal for two to be delivered today for tonight's dinner.' She looked at the name on the delivery note. 'Professor Cressida Davenport. Isn't she the clever lady who's helping Inspector Jack to catch the serial killer?'

'That's right. She's a really nice person who's had a few health problems lately. Normally, I wouldn't accept a late booking at this time of year, but she's more of a friend than a customer.' Corrie had stayed late the previous evening to get it finished.

'I expect she and her hubby are celebrating something. Maybe it's their wedding anniversary.' Carlene thought it was lovely that old people still did romantic things. After all, Professor Davenport had to be at least thirty-five, and her husband was even older.

Corrie looked at her watch. Ten o'clock. 'Could you manage for half an hour if I take it straight over, Carlene? Then I'll come back and help with the rest of the orders.'

'Course I can, Mrs D. No probs.'

* * *

Corrie packed the food into the refrigerated van in the loading bay outside Coriander's Cuisine. It was bitterly cold and the full moon, so bright at midnight, had now faded in the light of day. It hung behind the clouds, haunting and ghostly, like a disembodied soul. Corrie shivered.

Cressida had asked Corrie to decide the menu, so she had prepared some popular favourites. To start, vodka and cranberry cocktails with Gruyère puffs, then pan-roasted duck with a Grand Marnier glaze, fondant potatoes and Chantenay carrots. And to finish, tarte aux pommes with pomegranate ice cream. She drove to the Davenports' house, singing along to Christmas music from her playlist. Carlene would have condemned them all as 'music for dad dancing' but for Corrie, Christmas wouldn't be Christmas without Slade and Band Aid.

She pulled up in front of the impressive columned portico that displayed the name 'Davenport Hall' on a decorative plaque. This was the part of the job she loved, delivering food that would provide her friends with the romantic meal they wanted for whatever occasion they were celebrating. Corrie was as envious as she had been on her first visit to the Davenports in October. It was such a gorgeous house surrounded by beautiful woodlands, secluded without being too remote. She smiled to herself. She'd been a guest then. Now she was just the delivery driver.

She rang the bell several times but no one came. How odd. Cressida had said one of them would definitely be in to take the food. Then she saw the note, pinned to one of the two bay trees that flanked the grand front door. '*Key under pot.*

Back soon.' Corrie retrieved the key, thinking that Jack would not be happy with the Davenports' idea of security.

The inside of the house was as sumptuous as its setting, with opulent fabrics, thick carpets and furniture to die for. Corrie remembered the way to the kitchen, which was huge and had every top-of-the-range appliance. Wasted really, as Cressida didn't cook, but she recalled Oliver saying he dabbled a bit. She set the containers on the long central counter, then put the chilled food in the fridge. The pomegranate ice cream needed to go in the freezer if it wasn't to turn into pomegranate milk. She opened the door. It was crammed full of health food — quinoa burgers, butternut squash soup, meatless lasagne and what looked like kale smoothies. There wasn't room for so much as an ice cube, let alone a carton of ice cream.

It had been similarly full at the October dinner party and Corrie remembered Cressida taking her through the house to the garage, where there was another big double freezer for the overflow. She decided to put the ice cream in there and leave a note saying where it was. As she went past Oliver's study, she noticed a Santa Claus outfit, complete with hat and beard, hanging up in the corner. How lovely and festive. The Davenports didn't have any children, so Oliver must be playing Santa at a charity event or at the local hospital. She knew he was on a number of very worthy committees. She carried on through the garden room and conservatory into the garage. You could get lost in this house, she thought. Maybe I should have brought a bag of crumbs like Hansel and Gretel. She could feel the ice cream starting to melt.

There were no cars in the garage. Oliver would be at the bank on a Thursday morning. She imagined Cressida was either at the university or one of her classes. Corrie thought all that martial arts stuff was unhealthy. Exercise was one thing, but she couldn't see how learning to gouge people's eyes out then kicking them in the teeth made you a nicer person.

The double freezer was in an alcove, right at the far end. She tried to open the right-hand door, but it was locked.

Why would you lock your freezer? It wasn't as if anyone was likely to pinch their food. She rattled it a few times and finally, it flew open. But it wasn't a freezer, just a metal cabinet. The freezer part must be on the other side. She was about to close the door when something caught her eye. It was the photograph of the football team that had been on the front page of the *Echo*. Jack had a copy on the whiteboard in his incident room. She'd seen it when she delivered the food on the night of the Harvest Moon. These were the lads that the Moon Killer had been picking off one at a time. She imagined everyone in Kings Richington must be familiar with it by now. But why would the Davenports have a copy pinned to the inside of a cabinet in their garage?

She put down the ice cream and peered more closely. There was writing on it. It was hard to make out, as she'd left her glasses in the van and the garage wasn't very well lit. She had no idea where the light switch was. She'd probably get lost looking for it. Squinting, she could just see that someone had drawn circles around seven of the faces with a black felt-tipped pen. That was a bit weird. Why would anyone do that? And six of the seven were scored through with an angry cross that had gone right through the paper. The names of the six victims of the Moon Killer had been well-publicised in the *Echo* and on television. She couldn't remember them right now, but she'd be prepared to bet that they were the ones that were crossed out. It felt creepy, now, seeing them wiped out on paper, as well as in real life.

On the shelf in front of her, there was a computer print-out. She couldn't read it without holding it up to the weak shaft of light coming from the skylight. Damn! Why hadn't she brought her glasses? Normally they'd be on a chain around her neck, but she'd taken them off to put on her seat belt. She hesitated, thinking she really shouldn't be looking at this anyway. It was private and none of her business. But she picked it up. It was a spreadsheet showing the dates of the full moon, starting in March and ending in December. The names of the six dead men were typed in the next column.

It was a comprehensive record, with times, places and how they were disabled before they were killed. There were even copies of the pathology reports. Now Corrie realized what she was looking at and relaxed. It was part of Cressida's profiling work that she was doing for Jack. Yes, of course, that's what it would be. Nothing sinister about it at all. She was just being melodramatic.

Corrie felt guilty that she had been snooping. This was Cressida's business and probably confidential. It was almost certainly covered by intellectual property rights. In any event, it was nothing to do with delivering food. Once again, she started to close the door. But wait. What were those other things, pushed to the back at the bottom of the cabinet? Jack would accuse her of interfering again. Well, sod that — it had never stopped her before. In fact, her 'interfering' had achieved some quite spectacular results in the past. Carlene would say this was a 'shit or bust' moment. She pulled everything out, then immediately wished she hadn't. There was a black catsuit, some leather gloves reinforced with something heavy and, worst of all, a black leather mask, the sort that goes right over your head with just slits for the eyes. What was a cheap mobile phone doing in there? She knew both the Davenports had top of the range smartphones. A large butcher's knife lay underneath the gloves. Corrie picked it up. There was dried blood on it, and now it had her fingerprints as well. She recoiled in horror.

Maybe the Davenports were into S&M. She hoped it was that, and if so, it was none of her business. Live and let live was how she saw it, although she couldn't understand what pleasure people got from hurting each other. She had just about convinced herself that S&M was all it was, when something fell out of the pocket of the catsuit and onto the floor. She picked it up. It was a packet of tampons.

It was cold in the garage but the temperature dropped several degrees as the truth dawned on her. Unbelievable though it seemed, Oliver Davenport was the Moon Killer. It had to be him. Here was all the evidence. She had believed him to be a kind man — tedious, but kind. In fact, he was a ruthless, deranged serial killer. How could Cressida, a professor of psychology, be married to a psychotic murderer without realizing it? He was certainly strong enough to have been able to overcome his victims easily and he would have had the element of surprise. She doubted that any of them were expecting to be murdered by a banker, even if they did have an enormous overdraft.

She felt in her pocket for her phone. She must tell Jack what she'd found immediately, before anyone else got killed. But wait. Weren't there seven men ringed in the photograph? Only six were dead. Who was the seventh? She grabbed the spreadsheet again and squinted at it in the gloom. The seventh name on the list was Doctor Daniel Griffin. The date he was due to die was today, 12 December, the day of the full moon. But even more chilling was the place — Hambridges department store. That was where Bugsy had gone with Iris. Iris Griffin. So her son Dan *had* been on the football team! He and his wife had invited her and Bugsy for a lovely day out today, Christmas shopping. The two children would be there, too. She recalled Jack telling her that they had been sent a voucher for free lunches. What if Oliver had sent it, to make sure that Dan would be there?

Corrie felt sick. That explained the Santa Claus suit hanging up in the study. Oliver intended to go there dressed as Santa Claus and kill Dan, the last man standing. The store would be heaving and no one would even notice a second Santa Claus walking about among all the shoppers. He could pick off Dan whenever he got an opportunity. Trembling, she pulled out her phone. Before she could enter her passcode, a swift blow to the side of her head knocked her unconscious.

CHAPTER TWENTY-SEVEN

Back at Coriander's Cuisine, Carlene looked at the clock. It was just after eleven. Mrs D should have been back by now. The delivery should have only taken forty-five minutes at most. There were still loads of orders to prepare and deliver. She'd do it herself, but Mrs D had the van and the other one was already out with party food from Corrie's Kitchen and unlikely to return until late. Carlene called Corrie's mobile. It rang a few times then went to voicemail.

When Corrie had still not returned by noon, Carlene began to worry. It wasn't like Mrs D to go off schedule like this. Carlene had never known her do anything unprofessional, all the time she had worked for her. Maybe she'd had an accident in the van. The Davenports' address was right out in the country. She could be lying in a ditch somewhere, badly hurt. Corrie was the mother Carlene never had. If anything had happened to her and she hadn't done something about it, Carlene knew she'd never forgive herself.

She couldn't wait any longer. Carlene phoned Jack. As usual, she had to go through half a dozen constables before she finally got to talk to him. By then, she was really on edge.

'Inspector Jack, it's Carlene.'

'Hello, Carlene, how's it going at the food factory?' Jack was always pleased to talk to Carlene. She'd been with Corrie a long time now and they were both very fond of her.

'Fine, thanks.' Carlene was anxious to cut the polite chat and get to the important stuff. 'Is Mrs D with you?'

'No, she isn't. Was she supposed to be?'

'Well, no, but I'm a bit worried. She went out to do a delivery at ten o'clock this morning and she still isn't back. I wouldn't bother you, but it's not like her to go off somewhere without telling me.'

'Where was she making the delivery?'

'Professor Davenport's house.'

Jack did the sums. To the Davenports', then back to the catering unit. It shouldn't have taken more than three quarters of an hour, even if the traffic was bad. It was now ten past twelve.

'Have you tried her mobile?' Jack immediately realized that was a daft question. Of course she had. It would have been the first thing she'd thought of.

'Yes, five times, but it went to voicemail every time. Do you think something's happened to her?'

Jack was of Carlene's view that Corrie would never go off without telling someone, especially at Christmas when business was booming. A small inner voice reminded him of the times in the past when she had ignored his warning, become tangled up in one of his cases and narrowly escaped real harm.

'OK, Carlene. I'll go and look for her.'

Carlene was relieved. 'Do you think I could come, please? If she's hurt or in trouble, you might need some help.'

'Yes, of course. I'm going to retrace her journey from the Cuisine to the Davenports, so I'll pick you up there.'

Jack was aware that it was 12 December and still a full moon. Although he was convinced there would be no more murders, he was still cautious. He went across to DC Williams.

'Aled, I'm going out for an hour or so. Sergeant Malone has the day off to go Christmas shopping, so I'm leaving you in charge. If anything nasty crops up—'

'Like the Moon Killer, sir?'

'Yes, like that, and we need to deploy fast, ring me straight away.'

* * *

When Corrie came to, she tried to move but couldn't. As the mists cleared, she realized she was tied to a chair and as she couldn't move her mouth, she guessed she'd been gagged. Her head was throbbing. *Bugger*, she thought. *Somebody hit me!* Then, gradually, it all started to come back — the metal cabinet containing the spreadsheet of the murders, the leather mask and gloves, the catsuit, the knife and, worst of all, the tampons. The evidence that proved Oliver Davenport to be the Moon Killer. It all made sense now. The weight training, the muscles under his shirt. But why? What would make him do such terrible things? You'd have to be unhinged. But maybe he was. What if he'd been one of Cressida's psychology guinea pigs and she'd believed he was cured but actually, he wasn't? He had just been pretending to be normal so she would marry him and not give him away. He did seem normal to Corrie. It must be a Jekyll and Hyde situation, too complicated for anyone but the experts.

In the midst of all this fuzzy speculation, the really important issue stood out. According to the spreadsheet, Oliver was going to kill Dr Dan Griffin today, unless she could stop him. She had to get free and ring Jack. Her phone had been in her hand when she was knocked out. It would still be on the floor, over by the cabinet, but first she had to get rid of the damned chair.

It was a wooden fold-out garden chair. There were three others like it hanging up in the garage. They didn't look particularly robust. She felt sure that if she bashed it about a bit, it would fall apart. She rocked it backwards and forwards, hard, until it tipped over with a crash. But it didn't break. It didn't even splinter. If she got out of here alive, she'd tell the manufacturers what good quality their chairs were. Now she was lying on her back on the floor, still firmly tied to a chair. She needed to get free before Oliver came back to finish her off.

Maybe if she could get to her phone, she could wriggle one finger free and press the speed dial for Jack's number. She shuffled the chair, a bit at a time, over to where she'd dropped it. With enormous effort and a lot of swearing, she managed it. Her phone had gone, of course, along with everything that had been in the cabinet. All that remained was a piece of paper pinned to the open door. Written on it, in black felt-tipped pen, was one word.

Sorry.

* * *

Back at the catering unit, Carlene was waiting outside for Jack. She was really anxious. He could tell by her pinched face.

'Still no word, Carlene?'

'No, Inspector Jack. She must have had an accident. If the van had broken down, she would still have messaged me.'

'Come on, then. We'll go and look for her.' He didn't even want to think about the possibility of his Corrie being hurt, maybe badly. He'd seen enough RTAs in his career to know it can happen to anyone, no matter how good a driver they are. And Corrie was a good driver.

As they drove, Carlene was scanning the roadside for any sign of the van. It was easy to recognize because of the livery — bright green, decorated with herbs and with 'Coriander's Cuisine' on the side in bold letters. They didn't pass any accidents or broken-down vans. At last they reached the long, tree-lined drive that led to the Davenports' house.

Jack pulled up alongside the portico as Corrie had done some three hours earlier.

'Where's the van?' demanded Carlene. 'Do you think she delivered the food and then went on somewhere else? There wasn't another order on the delivery sheet.'

'Let's ring the doorbell and ask, shall we?' Jack was anxious now.

They pressed the bell several times, then Carlene just kept her finger on it, but although they could hear it ringing inside, nobody came to the door. He wondered if he should phone Cressida or Oliver to see if they'd taken delivery of the food, then gone out. He didn't want to unless it became absolutely necessary, as Corrie had said it was a special day for them. It could be that Oliver had taken his wife out and planned to come home to a romantic dinner, already prepared. They wouldn't want to be disturbed by a paranoid copper, panicking about his wife, when she might just have gone to the hairdresser's and forgotten to tell anybody. But realistically, he knew Corrie wouldn't have done that. While he was still considering it, Carlene had run around to the back door. He followed her.

'It's all locked up back here.' She had her hands cupped around her eyes and was peering in through the kitchen window. 'I can't see any lights. It looks pretty dark inside. I don't reckon there's anybody in.'

They walked all around the house, but everything was in darkness.

'Of course, they might both be at work. They normally would be at this time on a weekday,' Jack reasoned.

'It said on the delivery note that someone would be in to take the food,' insisted Carlene.

Jack could see that she wasn't satisfied, but there didn't seem any point in hanging about. He could go back to the station and get uniform to do an NPR check on Corrie's van. That would tell him where she had gone after she left here.

'Come on, Carlene. I think we're wasting our time.'

But she was already off to another part of the grounds. 'I think I'll just have a poke about in that wooded bit before we go.'

While she was gone, Jack tried to focus on all the innocent reasons why Corrie might be missing and not answering her phone. He couldn't think of any. Suddenly, he heard Carlene shouting.

'Quick! Over here! I saw a bit of green among the trees. If they'd had leaves on them, I'd never have spotted it.'

It was Corrie's van. Someone had driven it into the secluded copse, out of sight.

'Mrs D is still here somewhere.'

Jack and Carlene looked at each other, then they both began to shout.

'Corrie, are you here?' yelled Jack at the top of his lungs.

'Mrs D, can you hear us?' Carlene hollered. She ran to the house and hammered on the door.

Inside the garage, still tied to the chair, Corrie heard Carlene's voice. She tried to shout back but nothing came out from the gag beyond a muffled cough. She had to make some kind of noise or they'd go away. She dragged herself and her chair to the garage doors and with an enormous feat of agility for a lady of her generous dimensions, she managed to manoeuvre the legs until they were against the door. Then she rocked backward and forward so they made a noise against the metal. Carlene heard it and sprinted round the back.

'Inspector Jack! She's in here! She's in the garage!' She shouted through the crack in the automatic doors, 'Mrs D, is that you?'

It was at times like this that Corrie wished she had learnt Morse code. She replied with a couple of random bashes.

'Don't worry, darling,' shouted Jack. 'We're here now. We'll get you out. Don't go away.' He couldn't begin to imagine why she was locked in the Davenports' garage, unable to shout or let herself out by the front door. If this was the result of another of her ad hoc 'investigations,' she would have some explaining to do. But first he needed to see her, make sure she was all right. The up-and-over automatic doors wouldn't budge. It should have been possible, Jack thought, to force them up manually. It was what he did at home if there was a power cut. They tried several times, but it didn't work. He concluded that there was some kind of security lock holding them down. They needed to break it.

Carlene ran into the back garden and came back with a hefty spade.

'Let's try with this.' She rammed the blade into the gap under the doors and jumped on the handle. If I'd done that it would have snapped, thought Jack, but this was Carlene and it didn't. It smashed whatever mechanism was keeping the doors closed and made a big enough gap for Jack to push them the rest of the way.

They picked up the chair with Corrie still attached to it. Jack untied the rope and Carlene took off the gag. They both put their arms around her.

'Are you OK, Mrs D? I was so worried.'

'Whatever happened to you?' Jack was relieved to find her in one piece.

'Thank God you're here.' Corrie rubbed her sore wrists where the ropes had cut in as she'd struggled to get free. 'Jack, you aren't going to believe this. It's Oliver. He's the Moon Killer. I found all the evidence, but it's gone now. He must have taken it away after he knocked me out.'

'Oliver knocked you out?' Jack was astonished. 'Are you sure?'

'Yes, but never mind that now. Santa Claus is going to kill Dan. He might already have done it.'

'Who's Dan, Mrs D?' asked Carlene. She wasn't making any sense. It could be concussion.

'Dan is the son of Iris, Bugsy's lady friend. He's the last one on Oliver's hit list and they're all out Christmas shopping at Hambridges.'

CHAPTER TWENTY-EIGHT

Even though there was nearly a fortnight to go before Christmas Day, it seemed as though the entire population of Kings Richington was in Hambridges buying food and gifts. The store had clearly spent a lot of time and money on the festivities themselves. A massive Christmas tree, set in a giant pot in the basement, stretched up three floors into the roof space, where snowflake-shaped lights appeared to be floating down from the sky. The branches were lavishly decorated so that whichever floor shoppers were on, they could walk around it and marvel at the sparkle and glitter. Christmas music was belting out of the public address system and the staff were dressed as elves and snowmen. In the food department, there were free samples of mince pies and Christmas cake. Bugsy took a couple, just in case his blood sugar dropped before he got to lunch. He ate one and put the other in his pocket.

Iris had her arm through his, and the grandchildren, excited by all the festivity and thrilled to have 'Grampy Mike' with them, took it in turns to hold his free hand. It was altogether a magical experience and one that Bugsy would never forget — for a number of reasons.

'Where have Dan and Cheryl gone?' Bugsy asked.

'To buy some surprise gifts for James and Olivia,' Iris whispered. 'They don't get much chance to look around without the children.'

The visit to Santa's grotto was a novelty for Bugsy. He'd never been inside one before, not even as a child, and this one was particularly splendid. The outside was designed to look like an igloo, with strings of icicle beads hanging down across the entrance, where a sign told them they were at 'The North Pole.' There were large stuffed penguins all around the igloo, which amused Bugsy because there aren't any penguins at the North Pole. But James and Olivia were captivated, so he wasn't about to start boring them with a geography lesson. The inside was decorated to resemble Santa's living room, with a chimney and stockings hanging from the mantelpiece. Santa sat in his armchair in front of an electric log fire with a sack of gifts by his side. Bugsy watched, enchanted, as Santa gave each grandchild a present with promises to bring them what they wanted on Christmas morning, but they had to be good and go to sleep on Christmas Eve. Bugsy was amused to hear them giving Santa their address, including the post-code, just to be on the safe side. Maybe Rudolph had a sat nav these days.

The restaurant was on the ground floor and they had planned to meet there at two o'clock to miss the lunchtime rush. When Bugsy and Iris arrived with the grandchildren, Cheryl was there but Dan wasn't.

'He's popped back up to the toy department to buy a couple of those stuffed penguins that the children loved so much,' whispered Cheryl. 'He's going to take them out to the car and hide them in the boot. He said to order for him and he'd be here by the time the food arrives.'

They all opted for the full Christmas lunch as described on the vouchers they'd been sent, but when Cheryl produced these the restaurant manager didn't know anything about them.

'I'm sorry, madam,' he said haughtily, 'but Hambridges has never had any such voucher scheme for free Christmas lunches, not in all the time I've been here.'

From the look of the bloke and the speed he moved, Bugsy guessed he'd been here a hell of a long time.

The manager studied the vouchers more closely. 'They look like they've been printed on an ordinary inkjet printer. The Hambridges logo has been faked. Our gift cards have the logo *embossed* on them,' he said, snootily. 'I think someone must be playing a trick on you.'

Bugsy could see that Cheryl was upset and embarrassed. She kept insisting Hambridges had sent them. Who else would have done it?

'Never mind, love. Let's have the Christmas lunches anyway. It'll be my treat.' Iris looked gratefully at Bugsy and squeezed his hand, which was worth a lot more to him than a few lunches.

* * *

Dan was back on the top floor in the toy department. As he passed Santa's grotto, Santa Claus was just taking a break for his lunch, hanging a sign outside: *'Gone to lunch with Mrs Claus. Back at 3pm.'* They smiled at each other and nodded. *What a nice old guy,* thought Dan. *You'd have to be, to do his job. All those screaming kids, jumping on his lap and pulling his beard.* As Santa got into the lift to go down to the restaurant for his meal, another Santa was coming up the escalator.

At first, Dan couldn't find where you bought the penguins. Eventually, he found them right down one end of the toy department with a million other stuffed toys. He reckoned he'd better get a move on or his lunch would be cold.

As he hurried back past the now deserted grotto, he saw that the lunch note had been torn in half and lay on the floor. Surely Santa hadn't finished his break already? It was nowhere near three o'clock and there were no children waiting. He shrugged and headed to the lift to take it down to the restaurant. But he never made it.

The attack came from behind. Two powerful arms thrust under his armpits and hands locked behind his head, forcing his neck forward. As a doctor, Dan knew that a full nelson, applied correctly like this, could break his neck outright. It could also asphyxiate him or cut off the supply of spinal fluid to his brain. Whichever way it went, it meant brain damage or death. His attacker was dragging him backwards through the icicles into the grotto with consummate ease. This man was strong. He decided the best course of action was not to resist. Any sudden movement could be his last. He fought for breath, knowing that pretty soon he would lose consciousness.

* * *

Down in the restaurant, Iris and Cheryl were wondering why Dan wasn't back. They'd put a napkin over his lunch but as Iris said, it wouldn't stay warm much longer.

'Where can he have got to?' wondered Cheryl. 'He said he'd only be a few minutes.'

'You know Dan,' laughed Iris. 'Something will have taken his fancy and he'll have lost track of the time. He was always the same. Just like his father. Beats me how either of them ever managed to concentrate long enough to pass their medical exams.'

'I'll ring his mobile,' said Cheryl. But before she could get her phone out of her bag, Bugsy's started to ring.

'That's probably him now,' Bugsy felt in all his pockets and eventually found his mobile with half a mince pie stuck to it. But it wasn't Dan. It was Jack.

'Hello, Jack,' said Bugsy, full of seasonal merriment. There had been a festive silver hat inside his Christmas cracker and the children had insisted he wore it. 'Merry Christmas. Are the guys missing me already? Tell 'em I'll bring them back a Christmas pudding each.'

Jack's voice was urgent. 'Bugsy, listen to me. This is important.'

Blimey, thought Bugsy. *This doesn't sound good. What could have happened that had the boss all wound up?* He'd forgotten, in all the Christmas festivity, that it was a full moon. Surely there hadn't been another murder after all this time? And on his day off, too.

'OK, guv, I'm listening.'

'Professor Davenport's husband, Oliver, is the Moon Killer.'

'What?' Bugsy couldn't believe it. Mind you, it would explain how the killer had managed to stay one step ahead of the police. He must have been grilling the professor for information. 'Are you sure, Jack?'

'Positive. Don't ask me how I know — there's no time. We have evidence that he's gone to Hambridges today to kill Dan. He's wearing a Santa suit.'

If Bugsy hadn't known Jack better, he'd have thought this was all an elaborate wind-up, in very poor taste. But the boss didn't do that kind of thing. He was deadly serious. He got up from the table and moved away, so Iris and Cheryl couldn't hear him. 'But we've seen Santa Claus, Jack. He's an old bloke, short and fat. He wouldn't be able to fight his way out of a paper bag, let alone kill six men. And anyway, why would Davenport want to kill Dan? It doesn't make any sense.'

'Where is Dan now? Is he with you?'

'No, he went to buy some penguins half an hour ago, but—'

'Find him, Bugsy. Find him fast. I'm on my way with backup. I'll explain everything later.' He ended the call as the driver of the police car he was travelling in shot through a red light, blues and twos at full blast.

* * *

As soon as Jack had informed Chief Superintendent Garwood that they had a Grade One high-risk emergency incident, he had insisted on calling out the Specialist Firearms Unit.

'Won't that cause a panic, sir?' Dawes imagined what the reaction of Christmas shoppers in a crowded department store would be when a team of armed coppers burst in. 'We have no intelligence that the suspect has a weapon.'

'Remember what happened to the Reverend Toplady, Dawes?' Garwood winced, just thinking about it. 'The killer had a weapon then, didn't he? No, I'm not prepared to risk public safety.' He could imagine the *Echo*'s headlines if it all went tits up and he hadn't followed procedure. *Police risk lives of Christmas shoppers. Chief Superintendent accused of failure to deploy appropriate resources.*' It would be bad enough that the serial killer turned out to be the husband of the criminal profiler he'd brought in to catch the bastard. 'There's a killer on the loose in a store full of women and children, Dawes. Get over there and nick him.' And he'd picked up the phone to summon the SFU.

* * *

Inside Santa's grotto, Dan was fighting for his life. His assailant had him pinned face down and Dan realized he could be killed in a heartbeat — a grim irony. So far, his attacker hadn't spoken.

Dan summoned what little breath he had left. 'Why are you doing this?' he croaked. In fact, he wondered why he hadn't already been killed outright.

'Retribution.' It was a woman's voice. Harsh with rage and hatred, but a woman, nevertheless. 'I didn't want you to die without knowing why, and who, killed you. Retribution caught up with them all eventually — and you're the last.'

He had been half-expecting something like this since the killings started in March. But not from a woman. It couldn't be her, could it? He was becoming light-headed. Lack of oxygen to his brain.

'Cressy?' he gasped. 'Cressy, is it you?'

Cressida loosened her choke hold just enough for him to speak but not get away, like a sadistic cat toying with a helpless mouse. 'Of course.'

'Cressy, it's me, Danny Griffin. I was a year above you at school.'

'I know who you are,' she snarled. 'I knew who they all were. I always have.'

'Cressy, I didn't have any part in that terrible assault. I was the one who took you home.'

'It was rape, Danny, and you were there.'

'Yes, but I didn't take my turn, although they tried to make me.'

'*The only thing necessary for the triumph of evil is that good men do nothing.*' She forced his head further forward.

He was gagging, desperate to explain, to apologize. She tightened her hold, ready for the final execution. She had the tampon ready, in the pocket of Santa's tunic.

'Once you're dead, the last one, maybe I'll find peace.'

* * *

When Bugsy left the table and sprinted off without any explanation, Iris knew it had to be police work and something very urgent. It wasn't like him to behave erratically. She and Cheryl exchanged anxious glances. Then they heard the announcement, and members of staff came round, asking people to leave and directing them to the nearest exits. Iris and Cheryl helped the children into their coats.

'But, Mummy, why do we have to go?' complained Olivia. 'I haven't finished my pudding.'

James started to whimper. 'What's happening? I don't like it.'

Iris didn't like it either. Now both Dan and Mike were missing. What could it be? A bomb? A fire? She hoped they were somewhere safe, but suspected that, given their jobs, they would already be in the thick of it. As they made for the exit, people were starting to panic and by the time they reached the door, they were being swept along in a surge of terrified shoppers.

* * *

Sergeant Malone didn't wait for the lift or the escalator. He needed to get to the top floor as fast as he could. He took the stairs, three at a time, dodging between shoppers. They must have thought he was mad or drunk, leaping up the stairs still wearing the silver hat from his lunchtime cracker. He heard the public address system asking everyone in the store to make their way, calmly, to the nearest exit. That meant Jack had arrived and it sounded like he'd brought the cavalry with him. There hadn't been time to explain to Iris and Cheryl. He just hoped they'd manage to get the kids out safely.

When he reached the grotto, he saw that the penguins were scattered all over the place, as if there'd been a scuffle. He knew the real Santa Claus was downstairs in the restaurant eating his lunch, so the man inside the igloo had to be Oliver Davenport, the Moon Killer — the man who'd murdered six blokes and made the police look like idiots. Bugsy was ready for him.

He hurled himself through the icicles at full throttle and saw Dan, pinned to the floor and choking, with Santa Claus kneeling on his back. The 'living room' was in chaos. The armchair was on its side and the sack of presents had overturned, its gifts spilling out across the floor. Baubles and tinsel from the Christmas tree were strewn everywhere. Bugsy took one brief look, then shoulder-charged Davenport with all his weight.

When the hat and beard flew off, he saw that it was not Oliver but Cressida. In that split-second of total astonishment, Malone hesitated and the Krav Maga lightning combat kicked in. She winded Dan with a fierce punch to the solar plexus, then broke Malone's collarbone with a single chop of her hand.

'Sorry, Sergeant. I didn't want to do this. I rather liked you. But this is unfinished business.' She raised her fist to administer what would have been a death blow to his Adam's apple, when Jack burst through the icicles, followed by six armed officers.

'Cressida?' Dawes was dumbfounded. He'd accepted that Oliver was the Moon Killer but not Cressida. How could a woman have disabled six men with her bare hands? He soon found out. Undaunted by the guns and the shouted orders to lie on the floor with her hands behind her, she fought like a tiger, struggling desperately to complete her deadly mission by killing Dan.

It took four of them to take her away. She screamed at Jack as she went. 'He was the last one! I would have stopped. I'm not a serial killer. I don't fit the profile!'

* * *

'Bugsy, are you all right?' Jack grabbed his good arm and tried to help him up.

'Yes, I'm OK, but I think she's busted my collarbone. Oh, and look at that — I've torn my nice Christmas cracker hat.' He passed out.

From then on, it was mayhem. Paramedics surrounded Dan and Bugsy, both of whom were in considerable pain. They were carried off on stretchers to the waiting ambulances. Iris, Cheryl and the kids had been hustled out of the store amidst a shrieking crowd, who had suspected terrorist activity and believed they were fleeing for their lives. Iris eventually found someone in authority and asked what had happened to Dan and Bugsy. When she was told they'd been taken to hospital, she took the car keys from Cheryl who was still shaking and they set off in pursuit of the ambulances.

* * *

Much later, Jack came to fetch Bugsy from the hospital. He was now '*walking wounded*' but considered ill enough to be admitted.

'How is Dan?' asked Bugsy. 'I saw him throwing up in the corner after that bitch punched him in the guts and he must have some injuries to his spine.'

'The doctors say he's as well as can be expected, given what he went through. It was a hell of an attack and it's not as if he's a big bloke.'

'Could we go and see him before we leave?' Bugsy was still blaming himself for being unable to prevent it.

Dan was sitting up in bed with Iris, Cheryl and his children sitting beside him. James was feeding him grapes, bought from the hospital shop.

'How are you feeling, son?'

'I was lucky,' he croaked. His throat was damaged from Cressida's choke hold. 'It could have been much worse. You were brilliant, Sergeant Malone. I really thought I was done for before you burst in.'

Bugsy shrugged and winced as his broken collarbone moved. 'All in a day's work, mate.'

'I'll see you later when you're well enough to make a statement,' added Jack.

As they turned to leave, Bugsy pinched a handful of Dan's grapes with his good hand. 'I'm starving. Never finished my Christmas lunch, did I?'

CHAPTER TWENTY-NINE

Jack and Corrie were watching the report of the arrest on the late evening news. They each held what Corrie called a 'brandy bracer,' and it was a large one. Corrie reckoned it could be considered medicinal. They'd had a long and harrowing day and she still had a blinding headache.

'Of course, if you'd just delivered the food to the Davenports and left, you wouldn't have been whacked on the head and you wouldn't have a headache,' chided Jack. 'But no, not you. You had to go looking for trouble.'

'Thanks for that vote of sympathy, darling. And if I hadn't "looked for trouble," as you call it, Dan Griffin would be dead and I'd never be able to look Iris or Bugsy in the face again, knowing that I could have prevented it.'

Jack conceded that there was an element of truth in that. It had been a close call for Dan as it was. He realized that Corrie might also be dead if Cressida had decided to kill her instead of just knocking her out. It was a chilling thought and one he didn't want to dwell on. Thank goodness for Carlene. Like Corrie, she never gave up.

'Shall I fetch you some paracetamol?'

'No thanks, but you could get me another brandy.'

The news reporter stood outside Hambridges' spectacular Christmas window. Behind her, a merry Santa Claus was still soaring across the starry night sky in his sleigh, pulled by happy reindeer, and cheerful elves were still knocking out toys in their workshop. Somehow, it seemed incongruous after what had taken place inside the store that day.

The reporter's hair was blowing across her face in the biting wind and sticking to her lipstick. She was trying to speak while continually pushing strands of it behind her ears.

'Armed police officers today raided Hambridges department store and made a startling arrest. A police spokesperson confirmed that the man, nicknamed the Moon Killer since his reign of terror began in March this year, has been arrested. He is now being held in custody at a secure location, and police expect to charge him in the next twenty-four hours. He is alleged to have murdered six men. It is thought that he was attempting to kill a seventh when officers from the London Metropolitan Police Specialist Firearms Unit closed in and seized him. No weapons were discharged.'

'Poor girl,' said Corrie. 'She looks frozen. I can never understand why they have to send a reporter to the place where it happened, especially in bad weather. They could do it just as well from inside the studio.'

'They have to have an outside broadcast for a sense of location,' said Jack.

'But we don't need a sense of location. We all know where Hambridges is. You can't miss it — it's slap bang in the middle of the High Street and it's lit up like a, well, like a Christmas tree.' She chewed her lip. 'I'm assuming the police haven't released the information that the Moon Killer is a woman.' Corrie shivered slightly. 'Oh, Jack, I still can't believe it was Cressida. When I found all that stuff in their garage, I just assumed it was Oliver.'

'I know, darling. We both did. Perfectly natural under the circumstances. She had us both fooled. And the real bummer is that we brought her in as a criminal profiler, so she knew exactly what we were doing and could lead us in the wrong direction, which she did most of the time. She was very convincing.'

'Do you think Oliver knew?'

Jack was pensive. 'He loves her to distraction, so he may have been covering for her. But on balance, I think if he'd known, he would have tried to stop her. After all, if you love someone, you don't just stand by and do nothing while they systematically destroy themselves and other people as well. We're interviewing him tomorrow, so I think he'll tell us. If he did know, that will either make him an accessory or, if the CPS want to chuck the book at him, he could be looking at murder by joint enterprise.'

Corrie was silent, trying to make sense of it. 'Cressida and Oliver came here to dinner and we had dinner with them at their house. And all the time . . .'

'All the time, she was stalking men from a twenty-year-old football team and choking them with tampons.'

'Do we know why she did that — the thing with the tampons? Has she said?' Corrie wasn't sure whether she wanted to know the details or not.

'Not yet,' said Jack. 'She was unstable and screaming with fury when they took her away. I don't think she even heard me caution her. Garwood is going to interview her in the morning, after she's calmed down. Although I think the full details of the confession might be a bit rich for his blood.'

* * *

Next day, Chief Superintendent Garwood held a press conference, with Sir Barnaby sitting next to him, both in full uniform, buttons burnished and braid buffed. Inspector Dawes had been relegated to the end of the table — Garwood didn't want Sir Barnaby getting the idea that Dawes had been instrumental in bringing the killer to justice. Flash bulbs went off around the room.

'I am unable, for legal reasons, to name the person we have in custody, but I can say with all confidence that the so-called Moon Killer will no longer be stalking the streets of Kings Richington.'

There was the usual barrage of shouted questions that the press always asked, despite knowing they would not get answers this early.

'Why has it taken so long for you to catch this man, Chief Superintendent?'

'Is it true that the victims were all choked to death with tampons?'

'Has the Moon Killer been working in Hambridges as Santa Claus?' The journalist had been on the scene, Christmas shopping with his wife, and had glimpsed the police bundling a figure in a Santa Claus suit out of a side entrance and into a prisoner transport van.

'No, certainly not!' barked Garwood. The last thing he needed was a lawsuit from the store's actual Santa. 'Several interviews will be taking place today and a press release will be issued as soon as appropriate. There will be an opportunity for more questions after that. Thank you.' He stood up to leave.

'Is it true,' shouted a tabloid columnist, 'that the Moon Killer is actually a woman?'

Dawes suspected that the murmurs of shocked disbelief and derision that went around the room would have been very similar to those uttered by the crowd when Pope Joan gave birth during a papal procession. Garwood and Sir Barnaby left the conference.

* * *

The hospital had told Bugsy to allow his collarbone to heal naturally. The X-ray showed a clean fracture, they'd said, so surgery would not be necessary. They had fitted him with a simple triangular bandage to support his arm and hold the bones together in their normal position. He had painkillers to relieve what was actually a very painful shoulder, especially when he tried to move it.

Iris had insisted on taking him back to stay at her house. He had resisted at first, not very strenuously, but had had to agree that he would struggle to feed himself, which was always his priority.

'You can't possibly manage without help,' Iris had declared. 'It'll be much easier for me to take care of you if you stay with me. After all, it was saving my son's life that got you hurt in the first place.'

Bugsy helped himself to a second slice of fruit cake using his good arm. Iris made amazing cakes. Sometimes he thought he could happily live on just her cake.

'How's Dan?' he asked. 'I haven't seen much of him since I left the hospital.'

'They suspect he has a couple of broken ribs and something called a herniated disc in his neck. And Cheryl says he's covered in bruises. He can't talk much at the moment because of the damage that woman did to his throat. What a vicious person. She must be severely mentally ill.'

'I expect that's what her brief will say,' said Bugsy.

'Do you know why she tried to kill Dan? Was she one of his patients, or was it just a random attack?'

Bugsy did know but this wasn't the time to tell Iris. He felt Dan needed to do that. Obviously, she'd seen the press coverage but still hadn't made the connection between the football team from twenty years ago and her then sixteen-year-old son, since he'd given up football soon after. Dan's name hadn't appeared in the Echo, probably because as the only survivor of the serial killer, he was in a position to legally object to anything defamatory.

'Anyway, Dan's on sick leave.' Iris said. 'They've brought in a locum. And I'm taking time off until Christmas, so we can make plans about how to spend the holiday together. Is that all right with you?'

All right? It was almost worth breaking my collarbone, thought Bugsy, happily.

* * *

Professor Davenport was being held in the high-security wing of a psychiatric hospital. She had been interviewed by an independent psychiatrist with experience of serial killers. He had written several papers on the subject. He had also, inevitably, read many similar papers written by Professor Davenport herself. His risk assessment declared her too dangerous to be confined to a normal prison cell.

On the way to the hospital, Chief Superintendent Garwood made it clear how he wanted the interview with Cressida Davenport to proceed. He would have preferred it to have taken place back at the station, in the video suite, but he had been told that wasn't an option. In addition to the two officers who would stand either side of the door, the hospital had insisted on two male psychiatric nurses being present at all times. While he, Garwood, was interviewing her, Inspector Dawes and DC Williams — acting DS while Sergeant Malone was off sick — would be managing the recording machine and assisting with the questioning, if and when required.

That would be, thought Jack, if he forgets procedure and needs the correct form of words. An in-depth knowledge of PACE and the current Codes of Practice are essential in a critical interview such as this, and Garwood would want to get it right.

In addition, the professor would have her own defence lawyer present. He was one of the leading lawyers in his field — Oliver wanted her to have the best possible defence, money no object.

It was quite crowded in the room set aside for patient interviews. The two male nurses brought Cressida in and she sat down opposite Garwood.

'George, how nice to see you again. Are you keeping well? You look a little tired.' It was as if nothing untoward had happened and she was simply exchanging pleasantries with Garwood, as she had done a number of times before at the station. *This is seriously weird*, thought Jack.

Garwood was having none of it. He informed her that the interview was being recorded and that her lawyer would be given a copy of the recording. He motioned to DC Williams to start the machine, then gave his name and rank and those of the other officers present and asked the other parties in the room to identify themselves. Finally, he stated the date and time of the commencement of the interview and where it was taking place.

While all this was going on, Cressida looked mildly amused and totally unconcerned. It was as if she had retreated to a private and more agreeable world of her own. Garwood brought her sharply back to the present. This woman had already run circles around the police and made them look like incompetent idiots. He wasn't about to let it continue.

'Cressida Amelia Davenport, you are here because you have been arrested for the murders of . . .' He listed the names of the six men that he had written down in the file in front of him. 'And the attempted murder of Dr Daniel Griffin. Also, for an assault on Detective Sergeant Michael Malone occasioning grievous bodily harm. Do you understand?'

She smiled at him and nodded. 'Of course I do, George. And how kind of you to come in person. I know how busy you are.'

He ploughed on. 'During this interview, I will talk to you about your motives for these crimes and I will also ask you about anything else which may become relevant during the interview in order to properly establish the facts and issues.'

Go, George! thought Jack. He was doing all right, so far. He must have looked up the words and practised in front of a mirror, because he probably hadn't done this kind of questioning for years.

Garwood continued. 'How would you respond if I told you that items have been found in your home which have been identified as being used in the murders and which bear your fingerprints and DNA?' A comprehensive search of the Davenports' house had revealed that the items previously hidden in the cabinet had been removed and buried in the composter at the end of the garden.

'Well, George, I'd say that I should have kept them somewhere more secure, wouldn't you? But then I hadn't expected Corrie Dawes to go poking about in my garage while I was out getting some cash. She was just supposed to be delivering food.' She turned to Dawes. 'You see, Jack, it was going to be a romantic dinner for Oliver and me. I wanted to celebrate having personally executed those obscene excuses for human beings who didn't deserve to use up good oxygen any longer. Tell Corrie I'm sorry the food was wasted. She really is an excellent chef. She'll get paid, of course. She does understand why I had to knock her out, doesn't she? And as for DC Mitchell, well, I had to teach you all a lesson, trying to trick me like that. But I didn't kill him. You have to give me credit for that. I had a good laugh, though. Operation Moonshine that was supposed to be so hush-hush and there I was, sitting with you, while you told me all the details. It really was a hoot.'

Her lawyer put a hand on her arm. 'Professor, I must object. I really don't think you are well enough to be interviewed by the police. Let me ask for a—'

She shook him off. 'Nonsense, I'm perfectly fine. It's no use denying anything. They've got all the evidence. And anyway, I'm proud I did it. And with my bare hands.' She looked at one of the nurses. 'Edward, I'd like a glass of water, please. And then I'm going to tell you all a story.'

CHAPTER THIRTY

'Picture the scene, gentlemen. I'll make it easy for you, as I doubt whether any of you has much imagination.'

She's showboating, thought Jack. *If Garwood is expecting a remorseful confession, he's going to be disappointed.* Her attitude was hubristic in the extreme.

'It's a cold night with a full moon,' she continued. 'A young girl, barely fifteen, is hurrying across Richington Park. She's been to her gym class as she likes to keep fit. But tonight, she isn't feeling well. She has a heavy period and stomach cramps. She just wants to get home in the warm and lie down.'

Garwood flinched. Any talk of women's problems made him slightly queasy.

'She becomes aware of a group of young men behind her. They're boisterous and noisy, drinking lager from cans and jostling each other. One of them crushes a can and begins to kick it. They start an impromptu game of football, shouting and laughing. The can hits the girl's leg and they shout to her to kick it back. She ignores them and walks faster but they catch up with her and make a tight ring around her, laughing and jeering. There are seven of them, and in the light of the full moon, she recognizes each one. They are local lads, hoping to make Richington United's Under-21 team and have just finished their training.'

DC Williams swallowed hard and braced himself. He had a strong feeling he wasn't going to like what was coming next.

'The girl is scared and tries to break out of the ring. Wayne Jenkins grabs her sports bag and throws it over the fence. Toby Bryce-Jones pulls off her jacket and they throw it back and forth to each other, out of her reach. Then Hugh Toplady, the biggest and oldest of the disgusting animals, for that's what they are, forces her to the ground and pins her down. She is terrified and begs him to let her go. But now, of course, it's all about bravado, the alpha male needing to look cool in front of the beta members of the pack. Fragile masculine egos that can only dispel their sense of inadequacy and inferiority by demonstrating their superior strength over women. The Reverend Toplady, as he is to become, rips off her leggings and knickers and he rapes her. Brutally. She has a tampon inside her, but he doesn't care. Full of cheap alcohol and testosterone, the other cretins line up to take their turn. It was, gentlemen, as if they were merely practising for some harmless penalty shoot-out. The girl screams until, mercifully, she passes out.'

It was quiet for a long time. Garwood appeared unable to speak and kept sipping water to keep his nausea at bay. He seemed to have abandoned the format of questioning that he had intended.

Finally, Inspector Dawes asked, 'What happened to her next, Professor?' Since she was telling the story in the third person, he continued with it.

'When she regained consciousness, they had all gone but one — the youngest and smallest, Danny Griffin. He was sixteen years old and a year above her at school. He had retrieved her bag and jacket and he helped her into her knickers and trousers. Then he half-carried her home.'

'Did she go to the police?' DC Williams's voice was croaky.

She laughed, without humour. 'Bless you, Aled, of course she didn't. She didn't even tell her mother. When she got home, she had a bath and washed her clothes, which were covered in her blood. It was many days later that the pain of having a tampon pushed too far up inside her made her see the school doctor. Serious infection had set in and she had to go to hospital where they removed it surgically under anaesthetic. She told her mother she had done it herself, accidentally, forgetting it was there. Her mother, a weak, ineffectual woman, was embarrassed by the whole situation and chose to believe her, even though she suspected the worst after the doctors spoke to her.'

Garwood remained speechless. Slowly, he was beginning to understand the relevance of the tampon, which had never made sense to him until now.

'But she should have gone to the police!' insisted Williams. 'That's what we're for — to uphold the law and seek justice for anyone who has been attacked like that. They'd have rounded up those lads and made them pay for what they did.' Dawes could see that Aled was genuinely upset to be part of a law enforcement agency that hadn't done its job.

Cressida smiled at him. 'No, they wouldn't, Aled. They wouldn't have done anything. Think about it. For a start, the desk sergeant in Kings Richington police station at that time was Vic Walker's stepfather. He had high hopes of Vic becoming a star player. He was hardly likely to assist a silly young girl to land him with a criminal record. If it had ever come to court, you know exactly how it would have been. She would have been accused of encouraging them, wearing provocative clothes, and, since she had passed out, she really couldn't be absolutely certain who did what, could she? It was just lads' high spirits, and what was she doing out that late, anyway?'

Listening to her, Dawes feared that indeed might have happened. 'What did she do, Professor?' he asked. 'She sounds like an intelligent girl. She wouldn't have left such a terrible assault unpunished.'

'Well, I'm sorry to say she did, Jack. For a number of years. She tried to move on with her life and pretend it had never happened. The trouble was, every single moment of that rape came back to haunt her, every day. And at night, it became a recurring nightmare. Then, two years ago, she married. He was a kind, caring man with whom she wanted to start a family, but she suffered four miscarriages. She was finally told by her gynaecologist that because of the damage done to her cervix and womb all those years ago, she would never carry a baby to full term. This final blow was enough to push her over the edge of reason. The obsession with retribution took over the rational part of her brain. She looked to her expertise in psychology to try to understand and control the powerful urge she had to kill. When that didn't work, she studied the many ways it's possible for a strong, trained woman to disable a man using her bare hands. That proved to be much more rewarding.'

She seemed to make the transition, then, from someone telling a story to owning it. 'I inflicted sufficient pain and injury to prevent them from escaping, but not so much that they didn't know they were going to die. To say that I enjoyed watching them slowly suffocate to death would be an understatement.'

'Professor, I'm not trying to make any excuses for what was clearly an horrific attack on you,' said Dawes, 'but do you feel that the punishment you dealt them was commensurate with the crime they committed? They were very young men.'

She looked surprised at the question. 'Of course it was, Jack. You must see that it was my duty to remove these creatures from the human race. I'm not psychotic. I never lost touch with reality. I knew exactly what I was doing. That's why I was able to plan and trap my prey so cleverly.' She chuckled. 'You must admit, slicing off Toplady's genitals has a certain poetic justice. He bled buckets before I choked him with the tampon. Of course, I told him why. If he hadn't initiated the rape, the others might not have followed. Do you know, the bastard had the gall to ask for my forgiveness before he died?'

192

She emptied her glass of water and looked around the room at eight sickened male faces. Even her lawyer looked pale.

She stood up. 'I imagine you'll want to charge me now, George.'

It was very quiet in the car going back to the station. Garwood and Dawes, seasoned police officers, were nevertheless having difficulty coming to terms with the harrowing story they had just heard. DC Williams was so appalled he was virtually catatonic.

Eventually, Garwood spoke. 'I mean . . . a woman? A woman committed all those murders? How is that even possible, Dawes?'

'A combination of brute strength, determination and psychopathy, sir,' Dawes replied.

'I charged her, but of course it will never come to court,' said Garwood. 'They'll find her unfit to plead. Professor Davenport is clearly criminally insane.'

'The worst part,' said Aled, 'is that she seemed so normal.'

'Yes, but what's normal?' asked Jack. 'A person is only normal until they do something to make us think otherwise.'

CHAPTER THIRTY-ONE

The following day, the psychiatric hospital issued a statement.

A 35-year-old woman has been detained for further assessment after concerns were expressed following her interview by the Metropolitan Police. This woman will remain in hospital for an indeterminate stay.

The psychiatric assessor told Sir Barnaby that empirical research could not be relied upon to identify all risk factors. Risk was dynamic and could be affected by circumstances that could change over the briefest of timeframes. Since the need to protect the public outweighed the duty of confidentiality to the patient, it would need to be made clear to anyone who came into contact with Professor Davenport that she had a dangerous, incurable personality disorder. She was suffering from something akin to a Jekyll and Hyde syndrome, a fractured and unpredictable temperament. She had demonstrated a nature that was highly intelligent, educated and pleasant, while concealing an all-consuming rage that had come to the fore when she confronted the men she'd held responsible for her childlessness.

At Sir Barnaby's request, Chief Superintendent Garwood issued a press release stating that it was unlikely that the criminal known as the Moon Killer would ever be released. It seemed to him that as long as the murderer was locked away somewhere, the public didn't much care whether it was in prison or in hospital, as long as they would never be set free.

* * *

Once the identity of the Moon Killer became common knowledge, the press had a feeding frenzy. Reporters hounded Oliver Davenport to the extent that he had to leave his home and find alternative accommodation. He had been suspended by the bank that had employed him for the last fifteen years, in fear that the repercussions would adversely affect business.

Although both the police and psychiatric hospital staff were obliged to keep anything beyond the official statements and press releases confidential, these things had a habit of leaking out. Soon, the more lurid details from Professor Davenport's arrest and charges graced the tabloid headlines. They even had quotes about the castration of the Reverend Toplady and his early years as a sex pest. '*Should this man ever have been ordained?*' asked the headlines. Another long article questioned whether there was sufficient investigation undertaken by the church into potential vicars. The bishop was informed and had taken to his bed with stress. He had been planning to replace Toplady for some time, but this was beyond dreadful. He had no idea what the archbishop would make of it. In any event, he'd be sure to get the blame. He reached for the diazepam.

The manager of Richington United football team underwent a series of uncomfortable interviews with sports correspondents who asked him, quite openly, whether he was encouraging that kind of laddish ethos in the current Under-21 team.

Richington University experienced a drastic downturn in the numbers of students applying to study there. The psychology department was particularly hard hit.

Much worse was the effect on the families of the dead men when the reason for the serial killings was made known. The news coverage of the deaths had been intrusive enough at the times they were killed. It had abated after four months with no murders and the media had turned to other sensations, such as the infidelities of a Richington-based reality show celebrity. But the news about Professor Davenport threw everything up again in stark relief.

Wayne Jenkins's son, Ronald, had seen an opportunity in this for his widowed mother. If the press wanted dirt on his old man, they could have it. He negotiated a deal with the *Echo* for Sandra Jenkins to tell them what Wayne had really been like. Goodness knows, his father had never been any use to his mum while he was alive, why shouldn't she make a few bob out of the miserable git now he was dead? She gave them an interview describing how Jenkins used to knock her about, go with other women and how he'd put their daughter's boyfriend in hospital, after which they emigrated to get away from him. This resulted in a headline that screamed: '*Wayne Jenkins, the Moon Killer's first victim. Violent and immoral from an early age, says widow, Sandra, 39. Did he get what he deserved?*'

Camilla Bryce-Jones had no such desire for notoriety. When the reason for her husband's murder became public knowledge, she swiftly scooped up her children and went to live in their château in Provence. The extravagant house in Upper Richington, together with the cars and the yacht moored on the Thames, were left in the hands of her lawyers to be sold. Conversely, the effect of the scandal on the Bryce-Jones Investment Company had been negligible. It seemed that as long as the investors were making money, the historic moral turpitude of the now deceased company director was of little importance.

Winston Aduba's gym suffered badly from the news that the owner had raped an underage girl, even though it was twenty years ago. Parents withdrew their sons, arguing that it wasn't the sort of place for impressionable young men to spend their time. They had sent their boys to boxing training to keep them out of trouble, not to be influenced by a sex offender. Eventually, Errol had to sell the premises to a fitness club.

Up in North Shields, Bert Roberts flatly refused to believe that his precious son Joe could have done anything like the papers were saying. He must have got in with the wrong crowd. He was always easily led, right from childhood. Thank goodness his mother wasn't alive. This would have killed her. DS Billy Purvis of the Northumbria Police was just glad to close the file on such a sadistic crime. The murder was solved, even though he hadn't solved it. *Propa nasty business, like.*

Jenny continued to ply her trade from the cheap boarding house in the red-light district of Lower Richington. She had wondered, when it had all come out about how a rapist had been murdered in her room, whether it would put the punters off. It may have put some of them off, but mostly she saw an increase in business from the sick individuals who were turned on by that kind of thing.

* * *

At the end of any important case, Inspector Dawes would hold a wash-up meeting. The agenda was to discuss what had worked, what didn't work and what could be improved for the next investigation. It was fair to say that the MIT was good at learning from experience. However, the extraordinary nature of this case made it hard to identify anything useful to take forward. It was doubtful there would be another like it.

Everyone who had worked on the Moon Killer investigation was present, apart from Chief Superintendent Garwood. Apparently his 'ulcer' was playing up and he was at home, mainlining indigestion tablets and chamomile tea. Sergeant Malone was back, his arm in a sling, inside which he had stashed a couple of sausage rolls to keep his strength up. DC Mitchell's hearing had improved but he still had to wear the neck support a while longer.

The atmosphere around the table was one of stunned silence. There was none of the usual jubilation when a case was over — murders solved, killer in custody, everyone down the pub. None of that this time.

'She would have got all seven, if it hadn't been for Mrs Dawes and Sergeant Malone, sir.' This was a startled observation from Gemma, who was still trying to get her head around the whole ghastly business.

Dawes agreed. 'We were fortunate that she got careless towards the end, which is what happens to most serial killers. They start to make mistakes, leave clues. I think she originally intended to kill Dr Griffin during the Beaver Moon in November. She might well have succeeded, but she postponed it until December because she couldn't resist the challenge of attacking Mitch in the safe house, just to show us how clever she was. By then, she knew her psychosis was escalating and she needed to finish the task before it rendered her insane and incapable.'

'If we're looking for what worked, sir, the only CCTV footage we had of any use is the one that was outside Winston Aduba's gym.' Clive, the head techie, rotated his screen so they could see. 'I found this.'

There were thirty or so women in exercise gear, crowding through the door. The date was 18 May and the time six p.m.

'That'll be the Zumba class,' said Jack.

'That's right, sir.'

'And there's Corrie, my wife, with Mrs Garwood, Sir Barnaby's wife and Miss Catwater, Doctor Hardacre's assistant.'

'Yes, but look who's right at the back, sir.'

It was Cressida Davenport. She wore a grey, unremarkable jumpsuit and a grey fleece with a hood, which she had pulled over her head, making it impossible for her to be identified on the CCTV. But the facial recognition software on the police computer had made the match.

'She slipped in to kill Aduba under cover of the Zumba class.'

'I'd never have recognized her in that drab outfit.'

That explains, thought Jack, *why Corrie kept insisting she'd seen Cressida somewhere before, but couldn't quite place where.*

'How could we have got it so wrong, sir?' asked Aled.

'Professor Davenport is a very clever woman. She successfully tracked down the men she considered responsible for ruining her life, planned how and where she would kill them, and carried out the murders very efficiently. Had it not been for the tampon element, we might never have made the connection between the victims.'

'That's right, guv,' said Bugsy. 'We found possible motives for each of the victims to have been targeted. Jenkins was screwing over a drug baron, Bryce-Jones was insider trading, Aduba fixed fights for money, Walker took bribes from parents to get their sons into the Richington United team and Joe Roberts was buying hooky fish from fishermen who'd overfished their quota. Hooky fish.' He grinned. 'Did you see what I did there?'

Trust Bugsy to lift the gloom, thought Jack. The team worked much better when he was there. His approach was always to 'follow the money,' and very often, he was right. Except on this occasion. The grisly motive had had nothing to do with cash.

'What about the vicar, Sarge?' asked Aled. 'Who else did we have in the frame for wanting him dead?'

'Dunno, son. He'd been something of a shag bandit in his day. One of his conquests might have come back to wreak revenge. Come to think of it, that's more or less what did happen. In any event, if the professor hadn't stamped her identity on each one of them, chances are we'd have investigated them all as separate crimes.'

'Instead of which, we invited her in as a criminal profiler so she could see exactly how much we knew, what we were doing and send us off in a different direction.' Sergeant Parsloe had never been convinced of the wisdom of it.

'Her psychological profiling was genuine on a number of occasions, Norman, although obviously we had no idea she was actually profiling herself. I think she was toying with us, giving us clues, confident we wouldn't pick up on them.' Inspector Dawes stood up and went to the whiteboard. He pointed to one of the bullet points from Cressida's report. 'For example, she said here that the killer had been working up to murder most of his life. In her confession, she said there hadn't been a day when she hadn't thought about the gang rape and planned her revenge.' Jack pointed again. 'And here, she said that a traumatic life event probably tipped the killer over the edge, resulting in the first murder at one a.m. on March 21. The day before, when the moon had been full at 9.43 p.m., she had been told she would never be able to carry a child. And she mentioned that the killer disabled his victims with just his hands and feet. She was especially proud of that, so she wanted to emphasize it. Her report may have been deliberately misleading, but the clues were there.'

'She also said the killer was a strong bloke with gender issues, that he could have killed others we didn't know about and he was most probably one of the team in the photograph. Then she fitted up Walker.' Bugsy brushed flaky pastry off the table. 'I never bought that bollocks about the tampon being a metaphor for life and death.'

'Wasn't I right about the connection between a full moon, tampons and menstruation that everyone found so hilarious?' asked Gemma.

'Yes, you were. We know it was a full moon when she was raped, and she told us she was menstruating. To her, a tampon seemed the perfect murder weapon. And she told each of them who she was and why she was killing them before they died.'

'She was right about the killer having no moral compass.' Simon Jackson had been very quiet. He was struggling with the fact that it was he who had recommended the professor, a woman he had looked up to and admired for her academic brilliance, her personality and yes — her beauty. 'Sir, I'm aware that it was my fault she was invited in.'

Jack waved a hand. 'Not at all, Simon. Nobody is here to apportion blame. We all agreed to approach her.'

'Yes, but that's what I need to tell you. It was Professor Davenport who first came to me and suggested I should mention that a criminal profiler might be able to help. She'd already killed three men by then. Obviously, she used me to get in and find out how much we knew. I'm sorry, sir.'

'Well, I doubt we would have suspected her, even if we'd known that at the time. The purpose of a wash-up, Simon, is to assess what went well and what didn't. We'll list that under "What we could have done better" and leave it there.'

CHAPTER THIRTY-TWO

It became clear that Oliver Davenport had known very little about the woman he had been in love with for five years and married to for two of them. Jack had come to interview him, needing to establish whether he had been complicit in the murders and if so, to what extent. An arrest and a charge of accessory to several murders could follow. He hoped it wouldn't.

They'd had trouble tracking him down. After the press had besieged his house and the bank suspended him from work, he had fled to a monastic retreat in the country. His brother was prior there and had offered him the peace and quiet and time to reflect on the terrible events that had engulfed him when Cressida had been arrested and charged. No phones, no television, no internet. People in such a retreat were completely cut off from the outside world.

Jack started gently. 'I realize this is very painful for you, Oliver, but I need to talk to you about Cressida.'

'Jack, are you sure — I mean, are you positive beyond any doubt that Cressida committed all those murders?'

'She has confessed, Oliver. Given us details which only the murderer could have known, and we have irrefutable evidence.'

'But why? I don't understand.'

Given that the press had published every sordid facet of the murders, in increasingly graphic detail, depending on which paper you bought, it was hard to see how Oliver had avoided the information. The television had been rather more circumspect with the unpleasant bits, but all the same, Jack thought he would have picked up the gist of it, albeit reluctantly. But then, he'd been in a monastery, so no doubt his brother would have been shielding him from the truth. Better to start at the beginning where it all began, twenty years ago.

'Did she ever confide in you about how she was raped by a gang of lads when she was fifteen?'

Oliver blanched. 'Dear God, no. Poor Cressida. Is that who they were, these men she is supposed to have killed?'

Jack dodged the question. 'Could you please tell me something about your relationship with your wife?'

'I'm not sure what you mean, Jack. You saw us together at your dinner party and at ours. I adore her. She is an amazing woman.'

'Had you noticed any change in her recently? Say from around March?'

Oliver frowned. 'That would have been when the doctors told her she'd never be able to carry a child. We desperately wanted a family and she'd had four miscarriages. Then, in September, she had to have a hysterectomy. Something very wrong inside, apparently. I don't know exactly what, I never asked. We never discussed that kind of thing. Corrie visited her in hospital. It was so kind of her. Of course, that drew a line under any hopes of a baby. Cressida was devastated.' It was at that moment that realization dawned. 'Was it the result of what those men did to her, years ago?'

Jack nodded. 'I'm afraid so.'

'Then they deserved to die! Men like that are vermin. Filthy, repulsive animals!'

'I have to ask you this, Oliver. Are you telling me you knew nothing about what Cressida was doing?'

'No, I didn't. I wish I had known. I'd have helped her.'

'What about the things Corrie found in that cabinet in your garage? Had you seen them before?'

'No. I thought it was just a freezer that Cressida used for food that wouldn't fit in the kitchen one. She liked to stay well-stocked. She didn't like shopping, especially for food. She mostly had it delivered. Jack, why didn't she get rid of those things? She must have known how incriminating they were. When she knew Corrie had seen them, why didn't she chuck them in the river or burn them? Why bury them in the composter, where the police could still find them?'

'I think she wanted to keep them because they were mementos of her retribution. To her, they represented justice. And by that time, I don't believe she was thinking clearly. Any rational thoughts had been overcome by her need to finish the job.'

'Poor Cressida. She must be so sick. But she'll get better, won't she, Jack?'

'Oliver, the hospital where Cressida is being treated, they need to speak to you. They've been trying to get in touch. There's no easy way to say this, but it's unlikely she'll ever be released.'

He broke down then. 'You know, Jack, her mask was perfect. They say that love and marriage can help you know someone. But you can never be really sure, can you?'

* * *

Jack went home early. It had been a sad and poignant interview and he needed to be with Corrie to restore his equilibrium. She could always do that. He'd shared Oliver's tragic world today. Now he wanted to return to his own happy one.

'You don't think Oliver knew anything about Cressida's murders, then?' Corrie was dishing up corned beef hash, one of Jack's favourites. She'd sensed he needed comfort food.

'I'm sure he didn't and that's what I shall put in my report. He made a statement to that effect. His lawyer is going to see if they'll let him visit her soon. But she is considered dangerous. *"Cunning, manipulative and incurably psychopathic"* was how the psychiatrist put it. No feelings of guilt, conscience or remorse, and all the while displaying superficial charm and glibness.'

'She's only thirty-five. She could live another fifty or sixty years. Will they keep her locked up all that time?'

'I expect so.' Jack poured them both a robust glass of Merlot. 'Is there any—?

'Brown sauce? I'll get it.'

* * *

Sergeant Malone was having supper with Iris. Steak and kidney pie, followed by apple crumble and custard. When Dan popped in with flowers for his mum, it was obvious that he wanted to explain how and why he had been one of the serial killer's targets.

'I'd been expecting something of the sort since the murders started in March.'

'But why?' Iris was shocked.

'Because I was one of the seven in the football team that assaulted Cressida Davenport that night. When the other six were murdered, one after the other, I assumed my turn would come.'

Iris was speechless.

'Why didn't you tell me, son?' Bugsy asked. 'I could have helped. It might have meant we could have caught her sooner.'

Dan nodded. 'Yes, I know that now, Mike, and I wish I had. But when there were three full moons and no murders, I assumed I was safe. I didn't want to alarm my family or draw attention to myself. I certainly didn't expect an attack to come from inside Santa's grotto and definitely not from Cressida herself, after all these years.'

Iris finally found her voice. 'Dan, did you rape that poor girl?'

'No, Mum, I didn't. But I didn't stop the others, either. I tried but there were too many of them and they were all much older and stronger than me. I expected Cressy to go to the police and that I'd be called as a witness. I'd have been happy to give evidence against every last one of them. But when time went on and I didn't hear anything, I thought Cressy just wanted to forget about it and get on with her life. It was cowardly of me, I know, but I suppose I was relieved.'

'You were only sixteen,' said Iris. 'I remember you coming home late with blood on your jacket. I scolded you because I thought you'd been fighting. It was her blood, wasn't it?'

'Yes. I helped her dress and I took her home. I made up my mind that night that I wanted nothing more to do with football if it allowed young men to think that kind of feral behaviour was acceptable.'

'And you decided to be a doctor, like your dad.' Iris was beginning to understand a lot about her son. There was some apple crumble left, Dan's favourite. Wordlessly, Iris spooned it into a dish and handed it to him.

After Dan had gone, Bugsy took Iris's hand. 'Are you all right, love?'

'Yes. It was just a bit of a shock, that's all. How long have you known that Dan was one of that gang?'

'Not much longer than you. We had a photograph of the Under-21s with names on the back, but Dan's wasn't there. It wasn't until Inspector Dawes's wife found a copy of it in the Davenport's garage with Dan's face ringed, his name and details of where the strike was to take place, that we knew. Then everyone sprang into action and the police raided Hambridges. The rest you know.'

'Will the police want to arrest Dan for witnessing the rape and not reporting it?' Iris was very worried. 'He has a good career and this could hurt him.'

'Not after twenty years. We may need to question him and take a witness statement just to satisfy the CPS. It will explain why he was attacked, but that will be confidential. He might have to appear in court if Professor Davenport ever goes to trial but that isn't very likely. Don't worry, it'll be OK.'

CHAPTER THIRTY-THREE

Christmas Eve in Coriander's Cuisine was a triumph. The orders had been in for some time, so the folk she employed had been able to keep pace with all the various festive meals and different dietary requirements and the orders went out on time. They'd had a request for a roasted sheep's head from an Icelandic family. The cooks got on with it and actually, thought Corrie, it didn't look quite as grisly as she expected, as long as you didn't look it in the eye. A sparkly tree stood outside in the lobby, where it wouldn't contravene the Food Safety Act and upset those nice environmental health people. The Secret Santa presents were waiting underneath, where they'd be distributed at close of play, which traditionally was six o'clock. It was then that Carlene told Corrie her plans for Christmas Day.

'It's like this, Mrs D. I know I've always spent Christmas with you and Inspector Jack since you picked me up out of the gutter and changed my life.'

'You weren't in the gutter, Carlene, you'd just lost a bit of direction, that's all.'

'Yeah, but look at me now. I've got a brilliant job that I love, a flat to die for and the best friends a girl could have.'

'I'm sensing a "but" here, Carlene. Why don't you just come straight out with it?'

'It's my friend Antoine. You remember I told you about him?'

'Yes, he's a sous chef at Le Canard Bleu.'

'Well, he's a bit more than that, actually. His parents own it and a couple of other French restaurants besides. They've invited me for Christmas Day and Boxing Day. They're going to cook me traditional meals that they have in France at Christmas. I thought it would be a good opportunity for me to learn about authentic French cuisine. I could bring some recipes back here for you to look at. We could open 'Chez Carlene,' another arm of the business, specializing in French bistro food. What do you think?'

Corrie's heart went out to her as it always did. Her pixie face was puckered with anxiety, for fear she'd upset the most important person in her life. But Corrie knew she wouldn't always be and that Carlene needed to spread her wings.

'I think that's brilliant, Carlene. You'll have a great time.'

'I'll be back for the New Year orders, natch. Are you sure you don't mind me spending Christmas with Antoine?'

Corrie smiled. 'Is he good-looking?'

Carlene nodded enthusiastically. 'Yeah, he's real hot.'

'And does he make you happy?'

'Oh yeah, and he's a bloody good chef.'

'Then of course I don't mind.'

Carlene pulled out her phone to message Antoine with the good news, then thought it would be better to FaceTime him. Corrie wasn't actively eavesdropping, but her natural curiosity meant she listened just a bit. She was amused that Carlene spoke to him in French and he spoke to her in English. They had obviously agreed to learn each other's language. Carlene's French didn't sound too bad, but poor Antoine was struggling to get his tongue around Carlene's strangled English vowels.

Corrie's heart soared. Business was good, Carlene was happy, Bugsy had a lovely adopted family and she and Jack were set to spend a joyous Christmas together, without any interruptions from the Moon Killer.

* * *

Chief Superintendent Garwood was scanning the *Echo* to see if there were any articles about him. Christmas Eve was always a slow news day, so the editor might have decided to print his usual scurrilous attack on the police in general, and Garwood in particular, to fill up the pages.

Cynthia stood over him, sipping a large goblet of mulled wine. The Christmassy scent of cinnamon, cloves and oranges wafted down. 'What are you reading, George?'

'Nothing. This appalling rag is full of the antics of reality stars and speculation about who is likely to win the final of some ballroom dancing competition. I don't know why we take it.'

'We take it, Georgie darling, in case there are any pictures of you, so you can cut them out and paste them in your scrap book.'

Garwood flushed. 'How many times must I tell you, Cynthia? It is *not* a scrap book. It's a photographic record of exceptional achievement. I like to keep track of the successes of the MIT to ensure Sir Barnaby doesn't miss anything.'

'Well, you won't be able to take the credit for catching the Moon Killer. That was down to Jack Dawes. I reckon it's about time he was promoted, don't you?'

'No, Cynthia, I do not! The man's a loose cannon. He failed to identify that the killer was a woman and a very dangerous one. He even invited her to join the team as a profiler, so she knew as much as we did and completely skewed the investigation. Then he set up a surveillance that cost a fortune and resulted in serious injury to a police officer.'

'Yes, but it was Jack and his sidekick who finally nicked her, wasn't it?'

'He may have "nicked" her, as you so eloquently put it, but it was a team effort and I am the Senior Investigating Officer of that team.'

Privately, he was thinking that if Dawes was promoted, he'd move on to another Specialized Homicide Squad and his absence would reflect very badly on the clear-up statistics in Garwood's unit. No, he wouldn't be able to support an application for promotion any time soon.

* * *

Iris Griffin and Bugsy were staying at Dan and Cheryl's house on Christmas Eve so they could be there to see the children open their presents on Christmas Morning. Bugsy had gone right over the top and bought them all the things he'd heard them tell Santa Claus that they wanted in the grotto at Hambridges.

It had been a fortnight since Cressida Davenport had broken his collarbone. It was mending but still sore. Iris helped him wrap everything, then she helped him into the Santa suit that he'd hired. Both Dan and Bugsy had a momentary flashback to when Bugsy had cornered the Moon Killer dressed as Santa Claus who, far from dispensing magic and sparkle, had been intent on killing them both. Bugsy couldn't help thinking that if Cressida Davenport had succeeded in killing Dan in November, as she originally intended, this Christmas would have been very different for them all. Fortunately, her need to show the police how clever she was had got the better of her. But none of that was anything to do with the children and both men had agreed that the terrible events shouldn't spoil the kids' Christmas. Bugsy was determined to do what he'd always wanted to do if he had kids.

First, he filled their stockings, hanging from the mantelpiece. Then he crept upstairs with parcels to fill the sacks at the end of their beds. Iris and Cheryl crept up behind him trying not to giggle, taking pictures on their phones to show James and Olivia next day, just to prove that Santa really had come.

After Dan and Cheryl went to bed, Iris and Bugsy sat by the twinkling lights of the Christmas tree, sipping mulled wine and eating Iris's homemade mince pies. Bugsy thought he'd had four, but no one was counting. He'd bought a special present for Iris. He was a little nervous, hoping he hadn't overstepped the mark. Before he bought it, he'd run the idea past Mrs D. She'd said, *"Go for it, Bugsy. Faint heart and all that."* So he had, and now the gift was under the tree. He couldn't wait until the morning. He would give it to her now, while they were alone.

Bugsy watched Iris's face carefully as she opened the small box. It contained a solitaire diamond ring. Nothing flashy, but genuine and unpretentious, like Iris. All the years he'd spent as a copper had taught him to read faces and he reckoned he could tell a lot from expressions. He'd know if it had been a mistake.

Her face lit up with sheer joy. 'Mike, it's beautiful. Thank you so much. Is this what I think it is . . . ?'

Bugsy took her left hand and slipped it on the third finger. Then he kissed her, too full of emotion to speak. *What an old fool*, he thought. *At your age.* This computer dating lark had a lot to answer for.

Iris took another small box from under the tree and gave it to Bugsy. There was a key inside. 'I'd like you to move in with me permanently, Mike. If you want to, of course. That's your key to the front door and the rest of our lives.'

* * *

'Who was that on the phone?' asked Jack. It was late and Corrie had been chatting for some time.

'Carlene. She phoned to wish us a merry Christmas from Le Canard Bleu.'

Jack looked up from his Christmas present from Corrie — a new iPad. Now he could do all sorts of stuff, like play games and watch live rugby. It was brilliant. He'd been glued to it ever since he unwrapped it. He did a mental rewind of what she'd just said.

'Le Canard Bleu. Doesn't that mean the "Blue Duck?" Is that even a thing — a blue duck?'

'Oh, Jack, she's having such a great time. I'm so happy for her. Apparently, the French start their Christmas late on Christmas Eve. It's a feast called *Le Réveillon*. She said that means "wake up" because it goes on until the early hours of Christmas Day. Antoine's family really pushed the boat out for her. She's had oysters — she says they're like snot with lemon juice — then Coquilles Saint Jacques, foie gras, guinea fowl stuffed with chestnuts, and get this, thirteen different desserts. It's supposed to represent Jesus and the twelve apostles. They were eating until three o'clock this morning. Don't you think that's amazing?'

'It certainly is,' he said. 'I can put memos and events on my tablet and they come up on my phone. They can talk to each other.'

'Well, that's more than we can, apparently. I'm going to make eggnog.'

* * *

Throughout her career as a psychologist, Cressida Davenport had visited many psychiatric hospitals, including those caring specifically for the criminally insane. Never in her wildest imagination had she ever believed she would be admitted to one.

As Professor Davenport, she had written a widely read and much-acclaimed paper extolling the virtues of an open and rehabilitative setting that promotes patient recovery, patient safety and a good working environment for staff. This was no such place. She knew that, for her, there could be no rehabilitation and no recovery from her deepening psychosis.

She had been placed in an acute admission ward. This involved controversial measures, such as the temporary removal of her personal property, the searching of patients and visitors, the use of alarms and modern technology, and locking entrances to regulate those entering and leaving. In this hospital, there had been concerns over increasing violence and the high risk of assault faced by staff. In addition, it had been necessary to put in place stringent measures to protect patients from self-harm.

Cressida had refused permission for any visitors, including her husband. He had applied many times, only to be told that if she didn't want it, it could harm the balance of her increasingly fragile mental state. This had devastated Oliver. How could she not want to see him? On Christmas Day, he stood for hours outside the hospital, depressed by its grim facade, while snow built up on his raincoat and sorrow built up in his heart.

They told him that Mrs Davenport had been assessed by no fewer than three experienced mental health professionals who had all agreed that she was incurable and dangerous. It was their opinion that she could never be released to lead a normal life. Her once treatable psychosis had escalated into schizophrenia and the terrifying dissociative identity disorder. She now believed that she was two people: Professor Davenport, a well-respected but self-righteous university lecturer, and Cressida, a brilliant and cunning executioner of obscene rapists. She could switch identities at any time without warning. It was impossible to convince her that she had a multiple personality disorder, even though she herself had studied the condition extensively.

In her more extreme moments, which were becoming increasingly frequent, Cressida knew she had to get out of the hospital. She was needed in the outside world to redress the injustice of unpunished rape. She owed it to all the women who had tried and been ignored, ridiculed or worse, made to feel ashamed. But she couldn't escape while she was shackled to the sanctimonious Professor Davenport. She had to get rid of her and a plan was forming in her fractured brain.

CHAPTER THIRTY-FOUR

10 January. The Wolf Moon

Visits to the hospital shower room were closely supervised for high-security patients. The need for this was not just for the safety of the patient. It had been implemented in response to an increased demand for accountability by their relatives. There had been cases of liability for failure to provide supervision that met the standards laid down. The hospital had already faced two lawsuits for negligence. Given the high degree of risk in this case, Professor Davenport was accompanied by two nurses. They stood on either side of the door while she showered. Professor Davenport went into the shower room, but once inside, Cressida took over. She watched for an opportunity while she showered, and it came.

Screams could be heard down the corridor outside and cries of 'Help!' from a nurse. One of the other high-security patients had managed to break free from her minder and had grasped another patient around the throat. They were having a pitched battle and all available nurses on that floor were needed to break it up. Someone had pressed the panic alarm and a deafening siren was sounding.

At first, the nurse in Cressida's shower room did not leave her post, letting her colleague outside the door deal with the emergency. But when some other patients joined the brawl, a state of emergency was declared over the loudspeakers. The nurse glanced at Cressida, who was showering, quite calmly, and left to help restore order. She was only gone for a couple of minutes, but it was long enough for Cressida to reach outside the shower and snatch the plastic liner from the bin. She grabbed her towel and wrapped it around her, concealing the rolled-up bag between her legs.

Back in her room, Cressida waited until dark when the staff took turns to observe her. She knew she had to move fast if she was going to get rid of Professor Davenport for ever. During the changeover, she quickly pulled off her top and threw it over the CCTV camera in the corner. Then she removed the plastic bag from where she had inserted it. Her vagina might be all she had left of her internal genitalia, but it had served her well as a hiding place. She had concealed a tampon in the same way the previous day and hidden it under her mattress. Now, she took it out, forced it down Professor Davenport's throat, unrolled the plastic bag and swiftly put it over her head, twisting the long blonde hair tightly around her neck. Cressida knew she had to do it. It was the only way she would ever get out. The time was 7:10 p.m. Outside, in the cloudless January sky, the Penumbral Lunar Eclipse was clearly visible.

* * *

By the time the security guard whose job it was to monitor the CCTV cameras reported that the one on Davenport's room wasn't working, it was too late. Two male nurses went to investigate.

Davenport hadn't been on suicide watch, the official report said. They hadn't considered it necessary. Despite the assessment of her serious mental state, she had seemed docile and compliant. She had done nothing to alert nursing staff or the hospital psychiatrist that she intended to self-harm.

The management team was not impressed. *Try telling that to the lawyers when the next of kin sues us for negligence*, they declared. But when they told Oliver Davenport that his wife had committed suicide by suffocation with a tampon and a plastic bag, a lawsuit was the last thing on his mind.

* * *

Davenport Hall was up for sale. Estate agents were nailing the boards up when Corrie arrived in the van. The news of Cressida Davenport's death had spread rapidly across Kings Richington. The *Echo* had picked up on it straight away. Headlines were typically melodramatic: '*Dangerous psychopath dies in mental institution.*' '*Serial killer commits suicide.*' Mercifully, the manner of her suicide had not been released or no doubt, the editor of the *Echo* would have drawn all kinds of unsavoury comparisons with the deaths of her murder victims.

Poor Oliver, Corrie thought. What a terrible thing to read about someone you had loved very much. She had brought him some meals, thinking that the last thing on his mind would be cooking. But he wasn't there. The men from the estate agents didn't know where he'd gone. His lawyers were dealing with the sale.

* * *

The Agios Thallassos monastery sits precariously on a mountain peak to the southeast of Chania, on the island of Crete. It is one of the most inhospitable areas of the island. The rocky outcrop on which the monastery was built during the eleventh century, falls away into deep gorges all around, making it very difficult to access. The mountain is considered sacred, as legend defined it as the childhood home of Zeus. It had reached its cultural peak in the time of Homer, but its influence was also felt in the early Christian and Byzantine periods. The monastery had thus been established to follow the Rule of St Thallassos, a contemplative order prioritizing silence and prayer over everything else. In order to maintain its existence, the monks would take in supplicants from time to time to boost the coffers. They lived a hard, punitive life devoted to meditation and reflection.

It was here that Oliver Davenport incarcerated himself after the death of his beloved Cressida. He knew there would never be another like her and that for him, any future was pointless. He stayed there until he died at the age of eighty, a sad and embittered man.

THE END

ALSO BY FRANCES LLOYD

DETECTIVE INSPECTOR JACK DAWES MYSTERY SERIES
Book 1: THE GREEK ISLAND KILLER
Book 2: THE BLUEBELL KILLER
Book 3: THE SHETLAND KILLER
Book 4: THE GALLOWS GREEN KILLER
Book 5: THE MOON KILLER

Don't miss the latest Frances Lloyd release,
join our mailing list:

www.joffebooks.com

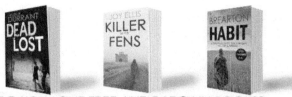

Made in the USA
Monee, IL
18 July 2021

73849954R00132